F
Ignorance

Are you living your life ... or existing for everyone else?

Maggi Holihead

This novel is entirely a work of fiction. The names, characters and incidents portrayed in it are the work of the author's imagination. Any resemblance to actual persons, living or dead, events or localities is entirely coincidental.

The author of this novel has worldwide copyright.

Prologue

'The future belongs to those who believe in the beauty of their dreams.' Eleanor Roosevelt

I don't know why I don't see myself as a successful writer as I have had one brief moment of success. Some say describing it as brief is a little harsh, but then again I have always been a little harsh on myself. It's the one time I nearly left Mike for a better life too.

The dreams of becoming a writer had started to haunt me; I spent a couple of years trying to write a successful Top 10, chart-topping, music hit. Once I started, the haunting dreams left me for a while and let me get on with my day-to-day life. Songwriting wasn't the easy fix I thought it was going to be. I wrote a number of different styles, hoping I would get lucky and produce a massive hit. Even writing one song in the forty minute bus journey on my way home from working in a different branch. Feeling proud, I did my usual routine; wrote a song or a verse of a song, read it several times, even singing along to the words, then put it away in the drawer of my dressing table. After a couple of days or so, I'd pick it up again to see if I still thought it was any good. Some were terrible, I'd feel that embarrassed I'd immediately shred the words. Embarrassed at the thought of anyone getting their hands on them and laughing at my pathetic attempts at writing.

A handful of songs were okay, or at least I thought they were each time I took them out of the dressing table drawer, I didn't have the desire to shred the words. I wasn't embarrassed and I even showed them to Mike. He never laughed at them, even though I knew he thought I was bonkers, but he read them to keep me happy. I decided to send them off to a music agent based in London. Mike took a photo of me holding the envelope before I got into the car and drove to the Post Office to post them by recorded delivery. Melanie found it highly amusing as I handed them over to her.

'What is it today then Lucy; the envelope is too thin for it to be your latest best-selling thriller,' she giggles.

'Actually Melanie, they are Top 10 music hits.'

'Get lost,' she laughs; quite hysterically I might add. She's even disappeared; I can't believe she's actually doing an on-the-floor laughing fit.

'Excuse me, but do you have an address where I can send a letter of complaint? The service here is terrible,' I say, trying to act seriously.

Melanie picks herself up off the floor.

'Sorry Lucy. Do you know what? I love the way you never give up on your writing, even though you know you're not that good at it,' she laughs.

'I'll take it that's your way of complimenting me.'

I hand over the money, pick up my receipt and put it in a safe place in my purse. Just in case the agency say they never received my work; and then the next thing I know there's a top 10 hit in the charts and it's *my* song. I wouldn't have the energy to take the agents to court. I've got electronic copies of the songs just in case it happens though.

'See you Monday Melanie,' I say, as I wave her goodbye. 'I'm off out for the day, hope you have a nice day in work,' I add.

'Thanks Lucy, I appreciate your thoughts,' she snarls.

Melanie and I are Best Friends. We promised each other that we'd be brutally honest, so if my bum actually does look big in a pair of trousers or a skirt, Melanie will tell me. She actually takes pleasure in being honest; it's a bit scary at times. I love her for it though and it's a refreshing change compared to the brown noses of this world who tell people what they want to hear in order to get somewhere in life. The brown-nosing is terrible where I work. I've never been one for it really. I just keep my head down and get through the day. I feel a little saddened that my heart has left my job and my life at the moment, usually I am a people person.

I actually feel good as I drive home from the Post Office. Every traffic light is on green. That has to be a sign that something good is going to come from my writing. I don't care what Melanie says, but I need her to keep my feet on the ground if I do make it big. As if, hey?

* * *

Six months have passed since that envelope left my hand; I hope Melanie posted it for me. I'm sure she wouldn't have placed it straight into the shredding machine!

On my way to meet Melanie for our usual lunch time catch up … gossip, people-watching, anything to distract us from the fact we work full time and lead dull lives. Distracted by vibrations, rummage in my bag and pull out my mobile phone. I don't recognise the number and it looks like it's a London dialling code. No one I know lives in London; I posted the songs to an address in London, but it can't be from them. It's ringing again, what do I do - do I answer it? What if it is the agent saying they like one of my songs? Maybe they're ringing to tell me not to send them anymore, that's probably more like it.

'Is that Lucy Boardman?' a male voice asks.

'It is.'

'Hi Lucy, my name's Lee and I work at a music agency in London. We received several songs written by you a few months back.'

'Oh, hi Lee.'

'Lucy, we like one of your songs and are looking at possibly using it for one of our top clients. We can't say 100% at this stage and we may want to change it, but we want you to come to London to discuss further. Can you get to London sometime soon?' he asks.

'I ... I'm sure I can. I work full time, so I'd have to book holidays; we normally have to give a month's notice though, unless it's an emergency. I'm waffling. Sure, I mean, of course I can come to London. Leave it with me; I'll ring you tomorrow if that's okay?' I ask.

'Great. If my phone goes to answer phone, just leave me a message. I've got your email address, so I'll send you some further detail,' he says, quite excitedly.

'Thanks Lee; speak to you tomorrow.' I try not to sound as if I'm about to explode with excitement.

'Speak to you tomorrow, Lucy,' he says, and then hangs up.

'Who are you on the phone to?' Melanie asks, as she stands next to me.

Trembling with nerves, I put my phone back into my bag. 'I need to sit down.'

'Are you okay?' Melanie asks, as she gets hold of my arm and guides me to the bench across the road.

'I can't believe it,' I say, as we sit down.

'What's wrong? Is everything okay? Are you okay?'

'I'm fine. I should be screaming with joy but I'm in shock. That was a music agent from London. They want me to go and visit them, to talk about one of my songs. I didn't even ask which one.'

'Well, that's fantastic Lucy. I mean I will miss you when I don't see you anymore at lunch time. But don't forget me when you make it big time.'

'Don't be silly Melanie, I won't be leaving work. If they do like my song and want to use it, it might be a 'one hit wonder'; even seasoned writers must have them. I can't afford to leave work, but it's a start isn't it? I wonder if I'll get a share of money each time the song is played?' I giggle. 'The only problem is they want me to go to London ASAP and I'm in work. I have to give a month's notice and I know Rick will let me have the time off if I tell him why, but it'll only cause more gossip if I don't follow the holiday process. Carol is already raising her eyebrows because Rick lets me work in other branches to try and stem my boredom. What am I going to do? I can't tell everyone the truth about what I need the holiday for as I don't want them knowing, not with the way I'm feeling about work,' I add.

'Throw a sickie!' Melanie cries.

'Shush, someone might hear you. I can't do that, something bad might happen to me,' I sigh.

'Don't be silly, when have you ever been off sick? Everyone does it. Just think about who goes off sick at your place; I bet Rick does at times, and I bet most of those are because of hangovers,' Melanie laughs.

'Just say someone sees me, or they try to ring me because they need to ask me something, and what would I do about ringing in sick? I'd have to get the 7 o'clock train to London. I can't ring in sick from the train can I?'

'Do you know what Lucy? You worry too much. What other option do you have?'

'I don't know. Rick's so disorganised, I could put a couple of days onto the holiday calendar and pretend it was always there and start reminding people I'm off for a few days next week. Or do you think it would be better if I booked a full week off? That way it would have to have been there all along; I can say it's been planned for months. Mike and I are going away for a few days!' I announce.

'So you think throwing a sickie was worse than that? A lie is still a lie, but I like it,' Melanie says.

Sickening stomach and thumping head; feel quite stressed as I walk back to work. What if someone else is off next week and I can't book it? Be glad when I've done the dreaded deed.

'Hi Lucy,' Rick says, as I rush past him through the door and into work. 'You're in a rush aren't you, if only you were this keen when we do your one-to-one's, don't forget yours is next week; hope you've prepared for it.'

'Next week? I'm off next week. Remember? You mentioned my one-to-one on Monday and I reminded you then; you said you'd reschedule,' I say, lying through my teeth; not even a drip of sweat or state of panic on my face.

'You're joking, I don't remember that. I don't remember seeing it in the calendar either. Then again, the weeks are flying by, aren't they? Maybe it was last month when I last looked at that. I'll have to get more organised. I'm just going for a sandwich, so I'll have a look when I get back,' he says, as he walks away.

'Lucy!' Carol shouts, as she sits at the reception desk. I've got about five minutes to get this holiday in the calendar. I don't look up at Carol; she'll want to chat.

'Sorry, can't stop,' I say, holding my stomach with one hand and the other over my mouth, as if I'm trying to stop myself from being sick.

Storm up the stairs and open the door to Rick's office, praying no one is in there. A drab office space, painted-grey walls and dull carpet. Holiday calendar which is a hard-back diary half-hidden amidst the overloaded desk. We should be using an electronic system, but Rick hasn't trained us on how to use it yet. Shit! Just realised we have to fill in a holiday request form and put it in Rick's tray. He then authorises it and checks that we have placed it in the book.

Holiday forms, holiday forms; there they are. Right, quickly, just scribble it down and sign. *Date of Request* - God, another lie. Well it's 15th April today and we have to give at least one month's notice. But I'll have to do better than that. Right, 14th February. Was I even in on that day? Yes, I was I remember because I love Valentine's Day and I remember gazing out onto the High Street as people busied past holding flowers and balloons. I actually had a brief moment thinking about something different to boring, crap work. Now where shall I put it? I'll just randomly place it in his tray, near the bottom. It's not my fault if he hasn't signed it and isn't more organised and has not shown us this new system. All done. My hands are feeling clammy as I push the door handle down and pull the door towards me to get out of Rick's office.

* * *

I'm not worrying about it anymore, as I'm sat on the train on my way to London. Mike and the kids wanted to come, but I might be with the agent all day and it would have cost too much. It's the first time in a long time I've enjoyed being on my own; watching the world go by as the train storms through each town and village. The rocking motion of the train feels quite comforting. An urge to go the toilet, but not brave enough … like something from a horror film, remembering my last attempt at entering a toilet on a train. I can still hear the stabbing music now in my head, as I remember opening the door and looking into the contents of the toilet pan.

Smile to myself as I look around, distracted by the man sat opposite; he must be in his early sixties. His glasses are perched on the end of his pointed nose, resting there as he reads his newspaper. Nostril hair stretching out, like desperate hands, pleading for help. I relax back into my seat; think of nothing for the rest of the journey.

Walk towards the hotel on Euston Road, look up at the dull buildings which are a pavement-grey colour and now mostly student accommodation. There's no hint of the amazing city I've just landed in and nothing to really admire as I walk, wheeling my suitcase behind me. I walk up the steps to the door of the hotel and into the reception area. No hustle and bustle in here which is good.

Finally, I'm sat in the reception area of the agency, feeling sick with nerves and my hands are clammy. The reception area is quite small; ten chairs sat around a large coffee table which is loaded up with magazines spread out across the top. The walls are painted post-box red; the pure-white gloss of the dado rail breaks up the darkness. Pictures of the famous clients they represent hang along the main wall. I only recognise two of them as they are in my age range.

'Ms Boardman, Lee's ready for you now,' the immaculately turned-out receptionist calls over to me from behind her desk.

'Thanks,' I reply, as I get out of my chair, picking up my bag off the floor and walk towards her.

The receptionist is sat there with her beaming, clinically whitened smile. Black hair is tightly scraped back into a ponytail. Her false eyelashes are fanning me as she sits there pouting and posing.

'Just go through this door here and up to the first floor. Lee will meet you at the top of the stairs.'

I walk through the door; my stomach is playing games with me again. It always does when I'm feeling nervous. Look up the stairs and Lee is stood at the top. He must be about my age; he has blond, spikey hair, shaved at the sides; obviously trying to keep himself fit and looking young. He dresses like a twenty-something, but he has an immaculate body, he can get away with it.

'Hi Lucy, it's great to meet you,' he says, with a huge grin as I reach the top of the stairs.

'You too Lee,' I say. I don't want to sound too over-excited.

'My office is through here; take a seat,' he says, as he opens the door to his office and lets me walk in first.

'Thanks,' I say, as I sit down and look around the small room.

It's as immaculate as he is; nothing is out of place. It's very modern with a lot of plastic and leather.

'Okay Lucy, we've spoken to our client, and he's been having a play around with your song. It's obvious you are not musically minded, and I don't mean that to sound as it does. You provided words only and not music with it, that's my meaning.'

'Yes, I agree. Don't get me wrong, I love music and I listen to music as I write. But there's no way I could accompany the words with notes or chords,' I hastily reply.

'As my client is in London, he wants to meet you. He likes to work closely with the people behind the scenes. He may want to have a session with you; play around with the words a bit. He likes to bounce off the people he works with.'

I'm focusing on the words 'session' and 'bounce' as Lee waffles on about how the industry works. He is right; I'm not musically minded, and not interested in the detail of how a song is created behind the scenes. I prefer 'session' and 'bounce', sat repeating the words 'session' and 'bounce' over and over in my head. I look at Lee but I can't hear any words. I'm definitely not listening to him. He's not making any sense to me. The door suddenly swings open and *he* is stood there; the musical genius; the sexy rock star is stood looking down at me as I squirm in my seat. He couldn't have heard my cry for 'session' and 'bounce' that's for sure. His forehead is glistening with heated sweat; he's dressed in fitted, black jeans and ripped, black t-shirt. His chest muscles and six pack are seeping through and crying out for attention; I can feel his heartbeat; it's in rhythm with mine. I've suddenly come over all hot and I have a strong desire; I want him and I want him to want me. I look over at Lee; he's not interested and is too full of himself and his own performance, as he continues to waffle on so dramatically, as if he's on stage in the West End. I look back at *him*. He's surrounded by smoke but I can't see a smoke machine. His stage presence is engulfing the room. He's pulling at his t-shirt with his right hand and his guitar is in his left. He throws his guitar across the room narrowly missing Lee as it smashes into the cupboards behind where Lee is standing. He rips his t-shirt away from his body to reveal an amazing torso; I immediately sit upright in my chair, place my right hand on my heart and grab my hair with my left, struggling to stay seated. His face is flushed with passion and his piercing, blue eyes are undressing me and look mesmerising against his dark complexion and hair. They are hypnotic and all I can do is look into them as he moves towards me. I feel completely helpless; there's nothing I can do as he reaches his hand out to mine.

'So what do you think then Lucy?' Lee asks, after his boringly, in-depth insight.

'I'm new to this so I'll just go with the flow,' I say, confused, and not having a clue about what I'm responding to. I feel flushed from head to toe and absolutely, completely relaxed. I look towards the door, there's no sign of *him*. There's no smashed guitar against the cupboards, Lee isn't being dramatic either, he's seated and probably has been all this time and is probably wondering why I am so slouched into my seat. I need to make sure I am being here now.

'Okay then; we'll go and meet him, have some lunch and then I'll leave you to it,' Lee says, as he gets up, gets his coat on and makes a call on his mobile.

I slowly get up off my chair, worried in case I leave a sweat patch against the plastic. Thirst dries my lips. I place the long strap of my bag over my head so that it sits diagonally across my body to spread the weight and keep my hands free. He opens the door to his office and lets me walk out first. We walk down the stairs and out of the door that leads to the reception area. Lee is off the phone now; I didn't even hear his conversation. He talks to the receptionist. She obviously fancies the pants off him. She's gazing into his eyes, twirling her hair as he speaks. She probably isn't even listening to his words, just watching his mouth move as he speaks. Oh my God, she's biting her lip now and has dribbled. And, to make matters worse, I've just burst out laughing. Where did that come from? Well it snapped her out of her hypnotic state of mind, says me after my episode in Lee's office. They both instantly turn to look at me.

'Sorry, I don't even know why I'm laughing. I must be feeling a bit nervous,' I say.

I'm still laughing as we walk out onto the bustling street. It doesn't help that Lee has his designer boxer shorts on that are higher than his designer jeans. He must be approaching forty years old and, don't get me wrong, it's great that he is still making an effort. I think it's just because I'm in a giggly mood, but the little things are making me laugh. I hope I'm not like this when we meet the famous client. Once I get the giggles though, I can't control them. Lee probably thinks I'm an idiot.

He opens the door of a very nice, chic, cafe bar and lets me walk in first. Once we get in, I stop in my tracks and let Lee lead the way. It seems quite laid-back; the waitresses are dressed in black trousers and t-shirts, paired with flat, black pumps. Even though there's no smoking, I can smell stale cigarette smoke. I can imagine before the ban, this place being filled with thick smoke, which would billow out of the doorway as soon as it was opened. The walls and ceiling are stained yellow, but it makes the place look more interesting. I can imagine places like this in Paris; it has that feel about it. There are old, wooden tables dotted around with well-worn, wooden chairs tucked underneath them. They are stained a deep orange. I like the fact they must fix rather than replace. It makes a refreshing change and I feel instantly relaxed. Lee stands there looking around.

'There he is; come on,' he says, as he walks ahead of me.

I nervously trail behind him, sheepishly hiding as someone stands up at the table he has stopped at.

'How are you doing?' Lee asks him.

'Glad to be back on home ground.'

'This is Lucy Boardman,' Lee announces and steps to one side to present me.

'Take a seat while I order a drink; do you want tea or coffee?' he asks, as I sit down.

'Coffee for me; black, no sugar,' I answer in a whisper, not feeling 100% comfortable. I'm totally out of my zone here with a famous person, and I feel a little embarrassed due to my earlier daydream. I'm quite shocked because he is very famous and has been around for the last twenty years or so. I'm shocked that one of my songs was good enough for him. But as I settle in, we get on like a house on fire. I think it's because my giggly mood is back and I laugh at everything he says. I think Lee is relieved; he's not taking my earlier fit of laughter to heart.

He must be a regular here because no one is interested in the fact he is sat here. He nods to the odd person here and there as people bustle past our table, but no one is staring or getting excited about him. We're just finishing off our coffees when this young, forty- something, blonde piece comes flaunting over to the table. I don't think there's much of her that is forty years old. Her beaming, botoxed face looks quite psychotic, huge lips smothered in bright-red lipstick. A warm-orange skin colour and huge breasts that obviously don't move when she does.

Wearing skin-tight, white jeans, she mustn't be bigger than a size six. The rest of her outfit comprises enormously high, red stilettos and a teeny, and I mean teeny, white top on with no bra. The gleaming-white clothing is striking against her orange complexion.

'I'm your biggest fan. Can I have a photo taken with you? It's always been a dream of mine,' she says, jumping up and down on the spot.

I'm sat open-mouthed, highly amused; it's brilliant.

She holds his hand; her false nails are daunting; they could slit his wrist. Her breasts are practically in his face. She might as well put her nipple in his mouth. I can actually see her nipple now, the right-hand strap to her top has fallen down to her elbow, which has lowered her top. My eyes start streaming as I watch them stand up for a photo.

Lee is cursing me with his eyes as he has the camera forced into his hands by the orange one. He has to keep his hands still to take the photo. The orange one has now put her arms around the rock star's neck, with one leg wrapped around his leg. All she needs to do now is put her tongue down his ear. The thought of that is making me laugh more, and when Lee says 'smile' as he takes the photo, it makes me even more hysterical, I try and distract myself by looking down into my handbag, rummaging around as if I'm looking for something.

I hear Lee say he can't work under these conditions and I'm not sure if he means the hysterical mess I am or what. I hear the orange one asking him for his autograph, but she wants it on her right breast so she can go and get a permanent tattoo of it straight away. The best of it is that she wants it lower than her nipple. As he finishes his autograph, she squeals because he brushed her nipple with his hand. Lee has started to laugh and is now sat next to me. The orange one is too fixated on him and has managed to block us out of her moment. That's freaky in itself, I did hear her tell him that she heard he came in here quite a lot, but she'd never managed to see him, until today that is, even though she said she could spend up to ten hours in a day to try and catch him.

Things have gone quiet, so I look up to see what is going on; is he still alive? The orange one is writing something on his hand. The owner walks over and asks her to leave as he is in the middle of a business meeting and that she'd spent enough time with him. He is an international star after all. He is starting to look a little worried now, but she kisses him on the cheek, thanks him for the autograph and winks at him as she turns to leave. He looks exhausted as he sits down at the table. I scrape myself up off the chair and excuse myself. I'd best get to the ladies to check myself out.

As I look in the mirror, I am surprised. I don't look as bad as I thought I would. Brush my hair and tidy my make-up and put on some fresh lipstick, before heading back to the table. They are both still sat there. He is quite hysterical as they talk about it. I have calmed down and there is no more laughter left in me. I sit down, happy to listen to them.

'We've ordered you another coffee, you must be exhausted after that,' Lee says.

'Thanks. Are you okay? Is that normal in your walk of life? I ask.

'You're a breath of fresh air you are.'

'Why do you say that?' I ask. I can feel my cheeks warm, blushing with embarrassment.

'I've not heard anyone laugh like that since I was at school; that's proper laughter, you were out of control,' he smirks.

'I'm sorry about that,' I say, sheepishly.

'Don't be embarrassed; I love it. You saw that nutter for what she is. In my world, especially when I'm on tour, we get that every day and it becomes normal. Women constantly throw themselves at us, desperate to get me into bed,' he announces, quite cockily and so completely arrogant, I like it.

'How do you know she wanted to get you into bed?' I tease.

'She wrote her number on my hand and also wrote 'I kiss in all the wrong places'. She didn't even write her name though,' he laughs.

'What would you do if you were going to ring her? Would you say, 'Hello, we met earlier; apparently you are my number one fan and I'll be yours if it's true what you wrote on my hand. Oh, and by the way, what's your name?'

'Lucy Boardman, you are funny too,' he brazenly says, as he and Lee burst out laughing.

'Well guys, I have to go now. I'll leave you two to finish your coffees and then arrange to meet up for a session,' Lee says, as he stands up and puts on his coat.

The word 'session' is fixated in my head again. I look over at him and he is quite a dish. Not that I'd ever do anything; it's just a day-dream. Not that he would want to do anything with me anyway; who do I think I am for thinking that? He's an international star. I'm nobody compared to him.

'Okay Lee, it was nice to meet you. No doubt I'll see you soon,' I say, with a smile.

'Of course, Lucy. We'll see what happens with this song. We'll talk money soon too and I'll give you a ring or send an email to arrange another meeting,' he replies, as he shakes my hand and then walks off.

'I'll see you tomorrow,' Lee says, to him, as he walks out of the cafe bar.

I feel a little awkward, not sure if I should excuse myself or what, Lee's just left me here with him.

'Do you want another coffee, or glass of wine?'

'I'll have a coffee thanks,' I answer, and I don't know why I've asked for another coffee as I've not finished this one, and I can feel my hands tremble with the overdose of caffeine. I'm getting completely wired on coffee. At least wine would bring me down a bit and make me sleepy, but it's too late to change my mind now.

'I don't know how you can drink any more of that stuff,' he says, as the waitress places my mug of coffee on the worn-out surface of the table. I'm glad she's taken my other one away.

'I was just thinking the same, I'll end up as high as a kite if I have any more,' I laugh.

As he gets up to go the men's room, I frantically root around in my bag for a bottle of warm water I left in there from the train journey. I seriously think I'm overdosing on caffeine; the thirst is unbelievable. On the verge of going hysterical, I drink the contents of the bottle and place the empty bottle back in my bag. A passing waitress tuts as she realises I'm consuming something I've not bought from here.

'I'm hungry, shall we eat?' he asks, as he sits back down.

'Sure, it might drown out the effects of all that coffee', I say, as I pick up a menu from the stand that is sat in the middle of the table.

'Steak and chips for me,' I say, as I close the menu and place it back onto the stand.

'I like it. You're certainly not a lettuce-eating stick insect, are you?' he laughs, as he glances at the menu.

'I'll have the same,' he says, as he closes the menu and clicks his fingers for a waitress.

We eat our food, have a couple of glasses of wine and talk, laugh, and argue. We just click; it's like meeting an old friend I haven't seen for a few years but feel as if we've never been apart.

It's 10 o'clock before we leave; it's dark outside and the temperature has certainly dropped. I feel an instant chill across my body as we start to walk back towards my hotel. I quicken my pace to warm up my body and try my best not to make it obvious that I'm freezing to death. I could forget myself and snuggle into him, wrap my arms around his body and get inside of his coat, but I can't so I'll just have to speed up a bit.

The non-stop talking about nothing soon takes my mind off the temperature. My frantic pace to keep up with his long-legged steps also helps. Locked into each other's gaze and conversation, just the two of us.

'Well, this is my hotel,' I say, and stop in my tracks.

'Oh, that was quick,' he replies, as he takes a cigarette packet out of his inside coat pocket. 'Do you smoke?'

'No.'

'Lucky you; I'm gasping. You don't mind, do you?'

'Not at all,' I reply, it's not as if I'm going to be locking lips with him tonight is it?

'Good night and thanks for a great day,' I say.

'It was my pleasure, believe me. I've really enjoyed your company. I forgot what it was like to spend time with a normal person,' he whispers, and holds my hand, yes, *he* holds my hand.

Do I pull away? I suppose he's not doing any harm and some people are touchy, feely, happy people and don't mean anything sexual by it.

'I'm going to go to my room now; so, I'll look forward to catching up with you tomorrow for a session,' I say, and I can't believe I said the word session and have a silly grin plastered across my shameful face.

'Oh, okay Lucy, well, I'll look forward to spending time with you tomorrow; shame we can't have more time tonight,' he says, with a smile as he lets go of my hand. His warm, rugged hand. I can imagine it now, touching my back and making its way up to my shoulders and then around to...

'Where are we meeting?' I ask, as I snap myself out of my trance.

'My studio is at my house, so you can meet me there. I'll send a taxi for you in the morning. Shall we say 8 o'clock?' he asks.

I'm still in shock about the fact his studio is at his home. I just hope it's in his basement or something and not in his bedroom. Who am I? Pull yourself together. As if he'd even want to make a pass at you, Lucy Boardman.

'Eight is fine; see you tomorrow. Are you okay getting home tonight?'

'Of course; I'm 45 years old,' he says, as he walks away.

'Are you okay getting home,' I cringe to myself. 'Why don't you come up to my room and I'll kiss you in all the wrong places,' I laugh to myself. If that wasn't a come-on from me to him then I don't know what is.

I'm stuck solid upon the spot where he left me. Move Lucy; move before he looks behind and then thinks you want him. Move yourself now! I snap myself out of it and walk up the steps to the doors of my hotel. Head straight to the lift and go up to my room. I sit on the bed trying to digest the events of the day. I'm on a high. I lie down on the bed and imagine him being here next to me, but the thoughts soon disappear when I realise there's no rest in me after all that coffee. I decide to head down to the hotel bar. One vodka and cranberry won't do me any harm.

Drink ordered and sat in the cosy lounge, next to the window so that I can look out onto Euston Road. Pick up a newspaper that's been left on the table. Enjoying this time on my own; I don't want anyone to think I look lonely. I've just thought ... I haven't even rang home yet. Grab my phone out of my bag. I've had fifteen missed calls and six texts.

'Hi Mike, really sorry I haven't been in touch earlier, it's been a crazy day. Can you believe I've only just got back to the hotel now? I feel awful, are the kids okay?'

'They're fine, don't worry, as long as you're safe. I was really worried when I didn't hear from you, but knew you were going to be busy,' he says, and in a good mood too, which has taken me by surprise, so used to verbal abuse and nonsense.

'I'm fine; I've had a really good day. I met with Lee and he took me to meet their client and we spent the whole day in his company. I'm meeting him again tomorrow as he puts the music to the words of my song, so that'll be interesting. And before you ask, no I don't fancy him and no, I don't fancy Lee either. None of them are my type. Anyway, I've got you and I love you,' I say, as I roll my eyes.

'You know what I'm like; I'm really proud of you; just don't leave me behind,' he cries.

'Oh Mike, you know I won't. Anyway, I'm going now; I'm going to bed because I've got an early start tomorrow. Are the kids there?' I ask.

'They've decided to stay over at your mum's, helping her out with the garden. I'll ask them to give you a call.'

'No, it's okay; I'll ring their mobiles and have a quick chat before I go to bed.'

'Well, I love you and I'll look forward to seeing you tomorrow night,' he says.

'You too, take care, see you tomorrow,' I say and end the call.

I ring the kids and have a good chat with them; it's so lovely to hear their voices, to know they're happy and okay with me being in London, they are proud of me and glad I'm finally doing something for myself instead of running around after Mike like a little lost puppy, they're really excited. I say goodnight and we arrange to book a table for tea tomorrow night, for a good catch up. I finish my drink and get the lift to my room.

It feels weird being in a hotel room on my own. I'm thirty-six years old and never done anything like this before. A quick shower before going to bed. I set my alarm for 6:30 to make sure I look good and have breakfast before the taxi comes.

A terrible din; takes me a while to realise it's my alarm already. Unbelievable! My alarm is going off and it's 6:30. Spring out of bed and get ready. I'll be alright in jeans and t-shirt as he was very casually dressed yesterday, and he'll be even more dressed-down whilst we're in his home. As long as he is wearing clothes when I call. What do I do if he answers the door naked?

As I walk down the steps to the waiting taxi, he's stood outside having a cigarette.

'Morning,' I shout.

'Morning. Did you sleep okay last night?' he asks, as he smiles and he has the most magnificent smile I've ever seen, or maybe I'm flirting again.

'I did. I wasn't expecting you to be in the taxi.'

'There's a change of plan. I've brought my guitar with me. I thought we'd go and sit near the Thames as you said you found water relaxing and so do I. Seeing as we have this hot weather for a change, let's make the most of it,' he announces.

I am feeling quite relieved that we aren't going to his house and it *is* a nice day.

'Great,' I say, as I get in the taxi.

He stubs his cigarette out on the floor and clambers into the back of the taxi with me.

'Where's your guitar?' I ask.

'It's in the boot; it's big and clumsy when it's in the case.'

Sit back, relaxed in the seat; the middle seat is empty, but he's sat with his arm stretched out and the tips of his fingers are more or less touching my hair. I decide to ignore it and concentrate on the music. I'm over-analysing things now; it doesn't mean anything; I just need to pull myself together.

It's a completely different story in my head though. He grabs hold of me by my t-shirt; no, I have a blouse on and the buttons are pressed, so he rips it completely open and kisses my breasts with a burning, sensual passion. His warm arms wrap around my waist as he pulls me ever so close, forces me towards him so I'm lying down and he lies on top of me and starts to unbutton my jeans; or maybe I have a skirt on for easier access.

'What are you smiling at?'

'Oh, nothing!'

We're sat on a strip of grass, not far from the London Eye. Streams of people are walking by, but no one notices the fact that there is an international superstar sat down next to me. There are that many people with musical instruments down this stretch of water, that it's easy to stop seeing them anymore.

I don't know why they wanted me to get involved with this aspect of the song, as I don't have a clue. I don't know what chords of music are. I know a good tune though and this definitely sounds like a good tune. Apparently, he's been up all night playing around with the song. I wonder if that was all he'd been playing with. Whatever he'd been up to, it was good. He'd changed quite a bit of the song but that didn't matter to me though; I was just glad I'd been given a chance to get out of my world for a bit.

I'm a little bored now though. Checking the time, I'm shocked to see its two o'clock already.

'I've got to go; I didn't realise it was so late.'

'That's a shame. When will I see you again?' he asks, and his face is crossed between looking sad and more than slightly annoyed. Disappointed; that's it; maybe he's used to getting his own way and used to being preened.

'Well, I'm not sure; I know I have to meet with Lee sometime soon. I don't know any more than that though,' I say, still puzzled as to why I'd disheartened him. His uncomfortable reaction has made me feel uneasy. I suppose he's that used to people like the orange one that I can sort of understand why I am such a breath of fresh air to him. But I am just being me; I won't start treating him any differently than any other work colleague. Deep down, that's all he is to me. I don't have any more room in my heart for another man; I have Mike … well, I don't really have Mike, and a part of me doesn't want him either. Not one drop of me has yearned for Mike. And I have started looking at ways in which I can get out of our relationship. Mike is determined we are staying together for life, but I don't want to. Yet I don't want to hurt him either, we want to live our lives differently, I yearn for peace and a drama-free life. He wants to live his life around his next drink.

Standing up, I brush the grass away from my jeans.

'Oh, you are in a rush aren't you? I'll walk you to the tube station; which one are you going to?'

'I'll have to go back to Euston. I've left my suitcase in the hotel reception. I don't mind going back on my own if you're busy.'

'I'll come with you; I'm heading back that way anyway. I'll get us a cab,' he says, as he fumbles around, packing his guitar back in the case. I've got a sudden urge; I really want to pick up his guitar and launch it into the Thames ... I don't know why.

'Why don't we get on one of those three-wheeled taxi-bikes? I fancied trying one last time I was in London,' I suggest.

I can tell he doesn't fancy it; you'd think I'd just insulted his mother by the look on his ever-frowning face. He probably doesn't want to admit that he thinks he's too good to go on one; but he's forgotten he's with a normal, working-class person. I bet the other women he hangs around with would have given him a right slap across the face at the mere suggestion of it.

Race ahead where a couple of bikes are parked up, he still can't believe it when I flag one down and as we fly through London City, he looks quite horrified, especially when we become sandwiched between two big, red buses. Clinging onto his life, his guitar case; the tips of his fingers are white. Hilariously smiling; he needs to be brought down a peg or two. He soon smiles when he hears one of his songs playing and the music swirls within the city air, and feels the velvet of the seating; exhilarated with the wind running through our hair. The power from the rider's legs is unbelievable. We pull up outside the hotel, totally windswept.

He pays the cyclist and then struggles to get out of the seat. I rush up the steps feeling the heat of his presence following me as we walk into the reception. Feeling uncomfortable, I wish I'd said goodbye when we were stood outside.

The receptionist leads me into a store room to get my suitcase, and for a brief moment I almost forgot about him. Enveloped by a warmth as he stands closely behind, peering over my shoulder. The busy receptionist rushes out of the room ... my body almost aches for his as I pick up my bag and clumsily turn around. Awkward silence; sinking heart as I dare to look up into his navy-blue eyes.

'Are you okay?' I ask, wishing I hadn't. My heart is bleeding and a part of me wants to just shove him out of the way.

'I don't know?' he says, looking downwards like a naughty school boy does when he's stood outside of the headmaster's office.

'Just say it; I don't want to be stood here in silence for the next ten minutes or that receptionist will think we're up to something.'

Feeling panic-stricken as he takes my bag out of my hand and places it on the floor next to me. Confused, I don't know what to do; shall I look away? Maybe if I start to have a laughing fit it'll put him off; the receptionist will come flying in and I can make a run for it. There's no laughter in me though; it's never there when I need it, and it always comes when I don't want it to. Try to look away, but he whispers my name, and his touch just feels ecstatic and as he embraces me a little tighter, I can feel every tingling moment. Sink into his arms as I lose myself within his hold, knowing that I don't even kiss Mike anymore. And as our lips meet within a 'never want to stop kissing you' embrace...

'So, you were going to ask me something?' I say, as we pull away.

He starts laughing and hugs me again. 'You make me laugh.'

'Well, I don't know what to say; I wasn't expecting that!'

'Do you have to go home?' he asks.

'I do; I've got a family waiting for me and I want to go back home.'

'So I can't tempt you to leave that life behind,' he has the nerve to ask.

'No, sorry; I'm off now. Hope you have a fantastic time on tour,' I say, quite offensively.

'Can I see you again?'

'Maybe, but only as friends. I want my steady, normal life.'

He's getting on my nerves now; he's holding me up and he's obviously used to getting his own way, and maybe he just wants to play with me for a while like a new toy. I hug him as I gently position him out of the way of the door.

'Here's my email address,' I say, as I scribble it down. I'm being a bit sneaky now; I can't give him my mobile number; Mike would know. My email is the only bit of privacy I have.

Before he can say any more, I rush out of the room; shocked to see Mike standing there in reception. A steely stare. Catch a glimpse of myself in a long mirror; hair that definitely is not in its place, though to be fair it was from the taxi-bike ride. Lipstick that has been removed within another man's embrace. Storming towards me with his fierce manipulation I rush back into the storage room. There are boxes piled up as far as the eye can see and no sign of him, my escape, my desire. Hidden within fear and a multitude of cardboard boxes as the door slams behind Mike. Aggressive in his approach as boxes are punched out of the way, I'm practically screwed up in a ball as the stomach-churning stench of stale alcohol consumes the room. He grabs hold of me in the usual way, fiercely grasping my wrists as he shakes me out of my hold.

'Lucy! Lucy!'

'Lucy, come on! That bloody alarm. Get your shit together, will you?'

Hazy ... smog-filled dullness in a lifeless room; a lifeless life, as I dare to open my eyes, then my sense of smell and touch returns. Realising I'm stuck in this rotten room in a rotten relationship with Mike, gaze across, lifeless Mike lying next to me in bed. Disappointed that the Rock Star is not in my life. I was listening to his music; it helps me sleep and forget. Disappointed that I've dared to wake up and gaze into my reality.

I am a great believer that the most important relationship a person should have is with themselves. Make yourself happy; but what do you do if a person is preventing this happiness from shining through? Am I allowing this to happen; is this really happening to me?

What has happened to me and *my* life?

Chapter 1

'To live is the rarest thing in the world ... Most people exist, that is all.' Oscar Wilde.

This is it. This is the moment I've been waiting for all of my life. Here I am, stood outside one of the most fantastic hotels in London. Never in my wildest dreams did I ever think I was good enough to be nominated for the 'New Writer of the Year' award. Me, Lucy Boardman, from Merseyside. *Working-class* Lucy Boardman ... bring it on!

Here goes! My legs feel weak with nerves as I walk up the steps to the entrance of the hotel. I can tell it's an important night, even the doors of the hotel are opened for me, the doormen are dressed head-to-toe in red and gold uniforms.

'Jeeez! I'd have to be paid £100 an hour to wear that outfit,' says Mike.

'Shush! Behave! We're going to be sitting amongst some amazing people tonight,' I hiss.

'Well, you're certainly not going to be nominated for "Personality of the Year" tonight, now are you?'

'Sorry Mike,' I say, as I hold his hand, 'I would've laughed at them myself, but I've got to keep it together tonight. I know I'm not good enough to win the title - I'll go to pieces if I do. Can you imagine me up on that stage in front of everyone? I'll either throw up or wet myself laughing,' I sigh.

'Come here, you'll be fine; you're great,' he reassures me with a hug as we walk into the expansive reception.

Veering through claustrophobic crowds, slow-motion, feels almost against my will, difficult to breathe, tightness around my neck; desperately craving relief but unable to move my arms as Mike's embrace holds me tightly against him. Clinking, celebratory glasses, roars of laughter, piercing my ears....

I feel as if I need the toilet as we walk down the main hallway to the suite where the event is being held. I stop in my tracks when I see the ladies toilet sign on a door and pull away from Mike's embrace to push open the door.

'I won't be a minute.'

Instant relief, shaking hands pressed against my heaving chest as I gasp for breath, for freedom. Freedom from what, I don't know? I catch my reflection in the long mirror that's fixed to the wall above the line of wash basins. I look younger than I thought I did, which is a pleasant surprise. My deep, honey-blonde, bobbed hair frames my pale, fresh face. My red lipstick looks quite striking, making my lips look fuller. Slow, deep breaths, composed.

'Not bad for 36 years old.' Even my large, navy-blue eyes are sparkling tonight. I just wish I could feel more confident and all of the time.

'I feel ill Mike, I want to go home!' I cry, as I walk out to where he is waiting.

'No, you don't. Come on, I'll lead the way. Let's look at the board with names and table numbers on,' he reassures me as he takes hold of my right hand with his left.

'Let's have a look,' he says, as he runs his finger down the list of names. Tightness distracts me as I look down at my hand captured within his, with a controlled grip of authority that judders through my entire body. I feel confused, sickly in fact, as I look up at his face. Surreal atmosphere: uncertainty, as I realise he wants me to remain under his control.

'Can I help you?' asks a smartly dressed young man, bowtie, and all.

'Hi, yes, I'm Mike, and this is Lucy Boardman; she's been nominated for the "New Writer of the Year" award, and we're looking for our table,' he proudly announces.

'Okay, sir and madam, you're on table number seven, follow me.'

I can't look around the dimly lit room as we are shown to our table. I know that no one will be pointing their finger at me in recognition. No one will be noticing me as they 'people watch,' as I am an unknown. That makes me feel more comfortable to be honest. I just want to sit down, have a glass of water, and calm down a bit.

'This is your table here. You are a little early and it'll be another thirty minutes before most people start to arrive,' he says.

'We thought we'd find our table. Lucy's a little nervous, so it's best if we sit and relax before the room gets full,' Mike says.

'Good idea sir. There's water on your table and we'll bring out the wine within the next fifteen minutes but let me know if you need anything before then,' he says, with a smile as he walks away.

'Do you think it'll be okay if I take off my shoes? My feet are killing me,' I ask Mike.

'And you were telling me off for not behaving myself!'

Smile to myself as I flip off my shoes and stretch my toes. It was a bit of a walk from our budget hotel because we couldn't afford the price of this one. £500 for one night! Who in their right mind would pay that? By the time we paid £70 train fair, £60 for the dog to go in kennels … I wasn't paying any more than £200 for a hotel. Oh, and there's the outfit, the shoes, the haircut and colour. God, it doesn't bear thinking about; all for one night!

'What are you thinking?' Mike asks.

'Money, as usual; I was thinking about what we've spent for one night,' I sigh.

'Stop it! This is your night, and this is what you've dreamed of. If I had my way we would have found the money to stay *here*, so shut up!'

'Sorry, you're right, and I *am* worth it, aren't I? I keep forgetting.'

Waiters pushing trolleys; bottles of expensive, red and white wine. Six bottles placed on every table. Excited, enlightened face, the face of a lottery winner as Mike cradles a bottle of red.

'Great, I think I'll have a wine,' says Mike. 'Why don't you have one too? It will help calm you down a bit?'

Looking around, I can't believe I didn't notice how beautiful the room is. There must be twenty-five magnificent, huge, crystal chandeliers, hanging from the wonderfully sculptured ceiling. There's one above every table. Talking about the table, it's amazing! There are three different types of silk tablecloth, with luxurious silk napkins placed in front of each setting, neatly rolled into silver napkin holders. Each table has a centrepiece of crystal candelabras surrounded by fresh fruit and flowers.

I wish I had a table permanently set out like this one - just not on this grand scale. Instead, we've got into the terrible habit of eating our meals while we're sat on the settee watching TV. I tend to use the chairs around my table to hang wet clothes on to dry. There's a radiator next to the table, so it's great for getting loads of washing to dry overnight. As I said … *working class* Lucy.

'What are you thinking about now,' Mike asks.

'Oh nothing, I'm just admiring the surroundings. It's a magnificent room, isn't it?'

'It certainly is. I love the ceiling,' he says.

'Oh, you've poured me a wine.'

'I poured it ages ago.'

'How is the wine, you connoisseur, you?' I ask, as I watch Mike meticulously swirl it around in his glass.

'It's good stuff!'

I can tell it's going to be a busy night. The waiters are getting into position with their backs against the wall, arms folded in front of them. I'm sure there'll be some actors and actresses here tonight. A lot of books are being turned into films and dramas these days.

I watch the stage as the spotlight is turned on and directed to where the mic stand is.

'It's starting Mike! It's starting!' I announce excitedly and watch as he pours the last of the red wine into his glass, tapping the bottle against the rim. Dare not waste any!

I'm stunned to see that our table is full; I didn't even notice anyone sit down next to us. I don't recognise anyone and dimmed lights make studying people's faces quite impossible. Here goes, there's someone walking up to the stand; I don't recognise him though … everyone's clapping, he must be famous in the writing world, oh well, I'll soon find out.

'I didn't catch his name then, did you? I'm struggling to hear because of all the applause,' I ask Mike as I applaud too.

'What?' he says with a strained face.

'It doesn't matter.'

'What?' he asks, as he squints his eyes. Why is he squinting his eyes when he's trying to *listen* to me?

I wave my hand dismissively to let him know it doesn't matter. Everyone's standing up now. Great! I'm only five feet tall, so not only can I not *hear*, but now I can't *see* what's going on. I shrug my shoulders as I look at Mike. He thinks it's highly amusing that I have a six-foot-tall man standing in front of me. The six-foot man doesn't think to look behind him. Doesn't think that there might be someone stood behind, struggling to see. I don't want to draw attention to myself by standing away from the table. I'll just clap and nod in appreciation like everyone else.

Oh well, Mike's certainly enjoying himself, as he opens another bottle and pours himself another glass of rather expensive red wine. I can tell he's already had too much, as his teeth are stained black, and he's stood there with the biggest grin on his face, nodding and applauding with the rest of the table. His cheeks are rosy red in colour. They always go red when he's drinking. The colour rises upwards from his chest and neck. I use it as an indicator, and I know that once the redness reaches his forehead he's had enough. But that's the way he likes it.

His unruly mop of red hair has a thin outline of wetness running across the top of his forehead and down each side of his face. That seems to be another side effect of his drinking. He sweats ... profusely.

I cringe as he stands there, stretching his arms up in the air, yawning and nearly getting trap jaw in the process. He has two huge sweat patches, one under each arm. He's acting as if he's among friends, as if he's among his kind of people. I like that about him, yet I find it funny. Everyone's sitting down now. I've just realised I didn't put my shoes back on. It would have given me an extra five inches of height as well.

The crafty get! I just realised that Mike's swapped our empty bottle of wine for a full one from the other side of the table. No wonder he had that big grin on his face. Look at him sat there smiling; it's a larger-than-life, smug smile. I can't stop focusing on his teeth though. Is it me, or have they gone even blacker? He looks like he's all gums and no teeth!

'They're doing your presentation first - look it's on the screen, "New Writer of The Year," Mike says as he points.

'What? Oh God! Okay,' I say, as I stop focusing on the gums and turn to face the stage.

I'm going to pass out, I can't handle it. Come on Lucy, focus and relax, *focus and relax*. Taking a couple of deep breaths, I place my hands on my knees, to stop them from trembling and to wipe the sweat from my palms at the same time. I can't hear a thing. I'm not concentrating because I'm so bothered about the way I'm feeling. I need a slap across the face or something to bring me back into the room.

'Lucy … Lucy!'

I look over at Mike. 'What?'

'They've just had a picture of you, up on the screen. Fantastic!'

'Did they?' I mumble.

I don't want to look at the screen. I'm praying that I don't win, so I don't have to face up to the fact that, as a winner, I'll have to walk up onto the stage in front of everyone, and I don't even hear the names of the other nominees.

Everyone on the table has realised that they're sat with a New Writer. They're all congratulating me on being nominated, trying to reassure me that it's the nomination that counts. Even the six-foot man has noticed me ... *now*.

I can feel the sweat running down my back and I wonder if I've gone white as a sheet. I look over at Mike. He has a sweltering, feverish face as if he's just run a marathon; red eyes disappearing within swollen cheeks. He's clapping and smiling smugly at me; I'm sure his smile now stretches wider than his actual face. God, he's opened his mouth! Now I can see the wine stains on his *tongue*. And now he's standing up! Okay, okay, so I've been nominated. Anyone would think I'd won by the way he's reacting. They'll escort him out in a minute. I knew I should have stopped him from drinking the wine.

Everyone on our table is standing up now and applauding me. What an over-reaction! Don't get me wrong, I'm not being ungrateful about being nominated; I just think it's a bit much. I know they say everyone in the writing world is passionate, but their reaction is a bit over the top; they don't even know me.

Mike is trying to get me up off my chair! I like my chair; I like sitting on my chair. I don't want to get up in case my dress is stuck to the back of my legs with the sweating. My hands are clamped to each side of the seat, as I sit rigidly upright with nervous paralysis.

Even the six-foot man is trying to get me up off my chair! Mike's got my left arm and the six-foot man has gripped my right. Talk about invading my space; they're both pulling me upwards, trying to prise my hands away from the chair.

I come back into the room now and hear the chaos and the noise. I can hear Mike telling everyone on the table that I'm nervous, and don't like drawing attention to myself. The six-foot man has got the nerve to point out that considering I don't like attention, I'm drawing even more attention because I won't get off my chair.

Looking up at the screen I can see that the camera has got a close-up of me. Oooh, I can see that Weight Watchers has done wonders for my physique, as I'm finally yanked from my seat. For the first time in a long time, I can finally say that ... *I Look Good!*

I snap out of my daze and realise I've won! Oh my God, I've won! *I HAVE WON!* Lucy Boardman is the 'New Writer of the Year'. Yes! Yes, it's true!

I remove the six-foot man's hand from my arm; I look at Mike and give him a thumbs-up, then a big hug and a delicate kiss on the cheek. Don't want anyone telling us to get a room. Best keep it formal.

Yes, ladies and gentlemen, Lucy Boardman has arrived!

I practically run up the steps to the stage and glide over to the microphone stand, where a man is waiting with my award in his hands. I still don't know who this man is. I hope I don't have to say his name when I take the award. My dress is slightly clinging to my legs, but I don't need to worry, because *I Look Good.* Kiss him on the cheek as I take the award from his hands. Stand in front of the microphone, not looking right out into the audience; I don't want to pass out on stage. I'm just about to do my speech when I catch sight of Mike as he starts shouting.

'Lucy! Lucy!'

The wine ... I knew it! I knew he'd ruin my big moment. I really don't want to look over in case he starts walking up the steps. I can imagine him stood at the bottom of them, glass of wine in one hand and a half-empty bottle in the other. His shouting is getting louder.

'LUCY! LUCY!'

He's shoving me now! He must be stood next to me but I'm confused as I didn't *see* him walk towards me. He wants to steal my limelight – *bastard!*

'LUCY! LUCY!'

I've just realised he's not on my right side, he's on my left. How did he get there?

'LUCY! You fucking, useless idiot!'

'LUCY!' His voice echoes within the air around me and my whole body is being shaken, shaken to the core, with such vigour and intent. I can feel the tightness of his grip on each shoulder. I feel as if I'm being lifted up and thrown onto the floor … but I'm not landing … just falling; falling as if I've been pushed off the edge of a cliff. My arms are flailing. That's the only part of my body I can feel, as I try to stop myself from falling over the edge.

I feel tightness around my neck and I'm frantically grabbing … grabbing at anything. I manage to grab hold of large tufts of long grass, which stop my downward plummet. I feel completely panic-stricken and struggle to get my breathing under control. I can't see or smell anything. I'm blind with panic and I can hear myself screaming; yet screaming *within* myself rather than outwardly as if I'm unable to let the scream escape *outside* of myself. I'm not sure if it is because of physical or mental restriction, but something is definitely stopping me from showing any kind of outward feeling or emotion.

A sudden silence in the air releases me from wherever I've been held. I know I'm not in the *Hotel in London,* and I'm not quite sure whether I was ever actually there anyway. I don't understand and I can't see where I am, or even *who* I am, anymore.

The only thing I do know is that I'm no longer in my *Field of Ignorance.* I'm no longer lightly skipping through a field of buttercups and daisies, with the sun warming my face. The warmth of the sun used to feel amazing against my tired skin. I could sit in that Field for hours; just sit deep in thought and hide myself away. I would shut out the noise that was going on around me, as if I was in my own little bubble. A protective bubble that would surround me, and I wouldn't see or hear anything when I managed to climb inside it. I didn't like the chaos I was living in, and every now and then I'd get up and walk around my Field. I can still feel the tips of my fingers gliding over the top of the long, soft grass; it was waist-length, sort of comforting. I had been happily skipping or hiding in that Field for a long time; just skipping around in circles. Or I'd sit amongst the long grass and hide away, praying and hoping that no one would find me. It was my daydream field, even my hay fever didn't bother me there. Every now and then I'd look up, but I couldn't take in what was around me. I couldn't appreciate any beautiful surroundings or the wild-life. I felt child-like and helpless, and when I knew it was safe I'd sit and cry. The only thing I could see was the vast amount of long grass that seemed to go on as far as the eye could see. I didn't want to see beyond that. I didn't know how. But I do know I'm no longer there; not anymore.

I'm sat in a heap on the floor of what looks like a jungle. It's very humid, sickly-hot and I'm struggling to breathe. The air feels thin and sapped of all the life-giving oxygen. I can't take a deeply drawn breath; panic-stricken I sit gasping and my skin feels cold and clammy against the cloying humidity. There is a putrid smell of stagnation, and it's then I notice the swamp water covered in a thick film of green algae. The only movement is from the skaters as they dance across the water. There is a buzzing in my ears as small flying insects swoop around.

I look out across the swamp. The tall jungle trees look as black as burnt ash against the early morning mist as it rises from the water. They look solid and still, as they grow out from the swamp. The trees in the far distance look like they're floating in the air and are faded in colour. The whole atmosphere feels, and looks grey, in the morning light.

The sound of rock crumbling and cracking distracts me, and I look up to where my Field was. I can just see the tips of the grass sweeping over the edge of what seems like a sheer cliff-face. There is no going back. I wouldn't be able to get back up there even if I wanted.

I'm quite sure that I *don't* want to anymore. I am fed up trying to keep so many people happy, just skipping along as if everything is okay. I have to face up to the fact that it *isn't*.

So, here I am. I look around to see what has dragged me down from my Field. I can see Mike in the distance, over on the other side of the swamp. He is chopping down the thick, tangled, jungle branches that would stop me from completing my journey once I'd managed to get through to the other side.

Was he the one who had gripped my ankles and dragged me from the field? Or maybe he pushed me over the edge of it? I tried my best to stay there. I grabbed hold of the long grass as tightly as I could. I even twisted it around my wrists so that I could get a tight hold and hung on for dear life. But as I was being dragged down into the jungle below, I could feel the roots of the grass being pulled out of the soil that had been its home for so long. There was nothing I could do, but as I look up to the place from which I have been torn, I am surprised I haven't been hurt. Looking down at my feet, I see my good old, faithful walking shoes; the ones that help me escape from my day-to-day life, as they take me along the beach with the dog. I'm so glad I don't have my high heels on.

I turn to my right; tangled branches are preventing me from walking that way, or even standing up. The branches are entwined, bulky and solid. I push my fingers through the gaps and grip them to try to shake them loose, but they feel completely solid. I feel like a prisoner locked away inside this natural cage. As I look beyond the branches, I can faintly see the figure of someone sat on the ground next to the swamp. The figure is partly hidden behind the mist that is moving inland; it all looks eerie and still. There's no movement or sound, and even when I try to push against, or shake the solid branches, there's no noise, not a single noise, nor movement of any sort. Maybe this is a journey; maybe everyone goes through this journey in their life. Maybe it's a journey everyone *needs* to make when they stop listening to themselves, when they stop making *themselves* happy. Instead, they're busy making everyone else happy.

I can't speak out, and when I turn to my left, it's the same; the tangled branches have encased me where I'm sat and there's no way out, but through the swamp. I look out across it and see that the only respite through the exhausting journey is work. There are doorways going into the bank where I work, just randomly placed on mini-islands that protrude from the stinking waters. I realise that my life has been focused on work alone and nothing else.

I no longer have the energy to live my life outside of work; I realise that now. Even when I get home, I have to deal with Mike and his need to have a drink. I know he works hard too, but he's got into the gut-wrenching habit of wanting a drink every night. Looking back the drinking was affecting my life too. I'd sit there every night watching him deteriorate. I'd find it exhausting, so I used to go off into my Field, smiling as the sun warmed my face, living my life as if everything was okay, yet not realising there was a cliff-edge at the end of that Field.

I dip my foot into the putrid water, gutted that my walking shoes are going to be ruined. There are rope-like branches hanging down from the dreaded trees that grow out from the murky, rotting swamp. I take hold of a branch and my right leg sinks deeper, dragging me downwards. The putrid water feels as thick as mud; I know if I let go, I'll be lost forever. I have to be strong; I reach out with my right hand to grab hold of another branch that is dipping down. As I grasp it, I pull my body forward and begin to wade. Exhausted, I realise I no longer skip into work, I am wading. My legs are heavy as I try to place one foot in front of the other. I manage to pull myself up onto the first island. Slimy, stinking, grey muddying, and vile stench, as each grappling movement of my body against the swamp-bed uncovers a layer that has lain undisturbed amongst this still place for centuries. Covered from head-to-toe in a slick of oil, heaving stomach, wrenching from deep within my soul. Exhausted I try to make sense of where I am, and looking around I can see that this island is no bigger than about two square metres, with the ground covered in a mass of broken foliage that must have been shed from the jungle trees. There isn't much shelter and I'm soaking wet through my clothing. My hands are cut from the friction of the branches. My hair feels damp and limp from the humidity rising over the putrid water. I feel exhausted, both emotionally and physically. I look up at the entrance door into work and my heart sinks at the thought of having to pretend that everything is okay. I don't have a choice though; I have to work. The door looks decayed; my nails can peel back the painted surface of the wood, and my fingertips feel the crumbling centre. I sit picking at the outer wood, contemplating whether I should actually get up and open the door. I know I can't sit here all day, so I take a deep breath and trudge into work.

* * *

I'm sat in my chair behind the glass wall that separates me from the customers who visit us daily. I used to love my job; always enthusiastic, always smiling, always happy to do anything. I am a '*YES*' person. Now that my son is older, I actually work *more* than full-time now that the bank is open on Saturdays and late evenings with no extra staff. I am the *'YES, I'll work extra on a Saturday'* person; the '*YES, I don't mind staying an extra two hours after my shift because we are short-staffed'* person. I am the ever-pleasing, compliant, *'YES, I don't mind not having a life outside of work'* person.

But I don't want to be that *YES* person anymore, and as my first customer stands in front of me, I want to get out of my chair, get my coat and walk out through that dead and decaying door. I know I can't, and I know it's not the customer's fault. It's me ... I've changed.

As I serve the customers with my pretend smile, I just want to press the button that activates the emergency shutters; the ones that shoot up to the ceiling and close me off from them when they turn out to be robbers. I'd even get a thirty-minute break, because it takes fifteen minutes to reset them, and we'd have to close the bank while that was sorted. I know I'm being silly; I have to sit in this chair because it pays the bills. But I know that things have definitely changed, and I know it's ME that has changed the most.

I realise I'm alone on this island as I wait to finish work. I have shut myself off from those that are important to me. I can't even remember how or when it happened, but I know:

I am alone.

It's getting cold and dark as I'm sat here, and I can see smoke in the distance. I know it's Mike; he'll have a fire going as he takes a rest from chopping down the branches. He'll be having the time of his life in this new place; nothing to worry about but chopping and building a new home, having a shower in the waterfall that glistens when the sun touches it.

I don't like it here though. I've got to get off this island because I know there's a new life for me, once I wade through the swamp and make it out on the other side of the jungle. I know that my son will be sat there waiting for me, waiting to get his mum back. My mum and dad will be there, with friends and family, so why the hell have I been in that Field all this time? I am actually *glad* I was dragged out of it and forced to be in this new place to spend time looking at my life; the life *I* had created.

As I robotically bring myself back onto the chair, I check that my pretend smile is in place. I actually touch my face to make sure, because I no longer physically feel that it is there. I've just got to figure out how to feel the real smile again....

'I'm going for my break now,' I say, as I lock my workstation and get out of my prison of a chair. 'If anyone asks, I'm out for lunch.'

I escape onto the High Street where Melanie and I make sure we have our breaks now. She works in the Post Office at the other end of the High Street, and because we meet for lunch, we have to make sure we get out on time; otherwise, we let each other down.

We used to have a woman called Sarah who worked at the bank, and the others would call her rotten because she always took her breaks on time, and never went without, like we used to do. I would listen, though I never joined in; but I didn't stick up for Sarah either. I suppose it's because at that point I couldn't understand why she couldn't be flexible with her breaks; why she made sure she got what she was entitled to. Now I know; now I understand why it was so important to her. No doubt that now I'm the one who is being slated. They're probably talking about me now, but do you know what? ... I don't care!

I've also realised that Mike and I no longer give each other a break. We've become strangers who meet up after being spat out of work. We never talk anymore and I never listen to anything he has to say, and I don't know why. Though every night he sits there, drinking wine.

Because Mike didn't like being on his own, and because he needed me to be there even though *he* was only there physically, I found myself sitting there each night staring at the television, but not even *watching* it anymore. I think Mike felt that he was spending time with me by forcing me to stay in the room with him; the room where he loses himself and starts talking wine-fuelled nonsense every night. I can no longer listen to it, and I no longer have the energy to be in that room with him.

I can see Melanie walking towards me, waving her arms as she does. Anyone would think it was the first time I'd met her here. Her shoulder-length, thick, brown hair sits solidly against her long, narrow face. Her sharp, green eyes can be piercing and intimidating at times. We've started to walk one mile each day before we choose a bench on which to sit and eat our lunch. Calorie burning; calorie counting.

'Feels so good to get out!' she says.

'I know! I can't stand it either. I don't know what I'd do if we didn't get out each day.'

'Come on, I want to show you a dress I've seen!' She grips my arm and drags me towards a shop.

Chapter 2

'Fear is the main source of superstition, and one of the main sources of cruelty.
To conquer fear is the beginning of wisdom.' Bertrand Russell

Pain. A deep, throbbing ache; my neck feels really stiff, as if I've been sleeping in an awkward position, or in a draught. I'm almost too scared to open my eyes as Fear has consumed my life; Fear is another person who is constantly shadowing me. It seems to have stopped me in my tracks and I know I'm no longer living *my* life, but I don't know what to do about it.

Frozen air seeps through my quivering skin and into the density of my bones; sharpened wind wraps itself around my cold, hardened body as an aching realisation I didn't sleep at all last night drenches into my soul. The mind games stopped me and kept me awake, exhausted; tired eyes stinging, as I threaten to open them, realising I'm on the island; the first island in the swamp.

Engulfed, thoughts from last night; cornered, held ransom, as soon as I walk in from work. Mike holds me in a small space, knowing I get claustrophobic, but he'll trap me there within his strong hold. Or follow my every move; torment and poke me. I struggle free as best I can, but I have to be quiet in case my son comes home.

My only way out is to give him the money I haven't got or acknowledge his need. He'll let go of me then; let go and lose himself in his own world. The fear goes into a different dimension when he's drinking though; as I'm no longer fighting him; I'm fighting a more powerful force, a force that even *he* doesn't control. My whole life is revolving around him and his next desperate drink.

A hazy outline of darkness; disheartened, gaze towards the second island; it seems so far away, an impossible journey, almost like a distant memory. Distracted, I stare as Mike's half-submerged shell of a body disappears within the swamp water. Shudder, when my eye catches sight of the jungle branch; the one he was constantly poking me with last night. The one he uses to purposely keep me awake; to wear me down mentally, emotionally and physically. I couldn't get away from him, no matter how hard I tried. Frightening flashbacks, knowing he won't remember a single thing and won't believe me when I tell him what happened; he says it's all in *my* mind.

'You're just a stupid fucking idiot ... now get to fuck! Get to fucking bed.'

68

I hate him, I really hate him. The constant, verbal, abusive attacks are unrepeatable. A part of me wishes he would die in his sleep, and another part of me feels awful for harbouring these feelings.

No choice but to go to bed; racing brain as I storm up the stairs, wishing *I* was dead, wishing he would strangle me, so that I wouldn't have to put up with this every single night.

Petrified, not knowing what he'll do. I can't tell anyone; ashamed, embarrassed, fearful. My constant companion, Fear, stops me from doing anything about it. Fear also has a grip on my life; I'm imprisoned by Mike, his drink and Fear. They hold hands and surround me ... I'm stood in the middle of the three of them and I can't see a way out of this vicious circle.

Lying in bed, door ajar, creaking motion as Mike's shadow crawls up the stairs. He sits and spies on me and each time I open my eyes he's inched his way that little bit nearer. Motionless, staring, getting ever so closer; Fear huddled against me, whispering into my ear, telling me that my life is in danger ... but Fear doesn't tell me what my options are, or how to deal with this; it has me in a stranglehold, weighing me down as if I have to first push past that, before I can move on.

Hypnotic rhythm as Mike's chest slowly rises and sinks back into the depths of erratic breathing; a physical being, struggling to recover. Hold and pull my body; hide behind the wide trunk of the tree; flinching flashbacks from last night, as if last night was my last night.

'What the fuck are you doing? I know what you're doing,' he shouts; bedroom light switched on.

Lying in bed ... I can't face *this* routine, not tonight. Frozen, exposed skin as covers are ripped away from my body, enraged aura standing over me. Forcing me out of my curled-up foetal position, hands on each of my wrists. I swear he'll break my wrists one of these days.

That's when I made my way back to this island, I remember fighting my way here. I had to fight him; fight the bottle, writhe around on the bed, writhing in this swamp. That freezing, dirty, swamp water froze me to the core; I thought I was going to drown last night. Clinging onto the jungle branches was my only hope, but Mike would always pull me back, as I desperately, frantically, grabbed the branches. He had a strength that even the branches could not withstand.

The last thing I remember is clinging onto a branch with both hands, illuminated knuckle whiteness with the sheer tightness of my grip. The mud-like consistency of the swamp water made it difficult for him to pull me back; drag me back with full force. He kept losing his grip each time ... and gave up in the end. Placing each hand on my shoulders and shaking me to the core; completely disgusted with me.

Freezing, quivering chills as jungle wind darts into my empty and soulless body. An uncontrolled coldness; I don't want to speak or even look at him this morning. Dismayed, look at the bruising on my wrists and legs; dirty and awkward. I've got to pull myself together.

Enchanting, ghostly, white blanket as early morning mist rises from within the swamp waters. Gaze across as hazy sunrise desperately tries to filter through and break up the mist. Deep breath as I look across to Mike lying amongst littered, empty bottles and a wine glass still glued to his right hand; he's gripping it as if it's the World Cup trophy. Hypnotically watch as the empty bottles float away within the misty current, leaving behind the clearness of the damp morning.

Everything seems grey and lifeless ... the floor of the island is damp and slimy. My hands are practically cemented into the consistency of it. I look out across the water which is completely flat ... deformed reflections of blackness from the trees float on the surface. The black trees look fragile, still and stiff this morning. The trunk of the jungle tree is crumbling under the weight of my hold. I shuffle my body away from it. Suffocated by a feeling of dread as I look up at my bedroom door; knowing I have to stand up and walk in and get ready for work. I have to work. Look back at Mike's lifeless body and shiver as the cold morning wind strikes my back, like a knife being pushed through my spine. It's enough to make me flinch. The door creaks as the wind forces it open; it's rotting in the harsh jungle conditions. The paint is flaking, and the exposed wood is damp and crumbling. I'm almost too scared to touch it in case it completely disintegrates. I'll be stuck here forever, unable to get back to the land of the living. A part of me likes that idea; I could hide and stay here and not face up to everything. But those thoughts are dangerous, and this place is harsh ... I can't stay here.

Slowly stand and take hold of the door handle, look around at the grey, damp place I'm in. There's no sound or colour here; nothing. My hair feels hard; the mud from the swamp water has clung to my hair and dried like clay; I'll have to wash it before I go to work. Sneaking out of the jungle through the door, I need to get off this island in the hope I don't wake him, so that I can have a bit of time on my own before I go to work. Rest my racing mind and dust myself down.

I'm working in another branch today, covering for sickness and holidays. I feel a little anxious, but it also feels good to get on a different bus, to go in a different direction for a change. It distracts my mind, as I'm normally on autopilot because I know the route of my journey so well.

Obsessively gaze out of the window as the bus halts at each stop; near trance as I try not to make eye contact with anyone or make it obvious that I am looking at them. I like to check out the hairstyles and clothing that the women wear, as they patiently wait for their buses. It's amazing how some are very clean-cut with sharp haircuts and fashionable clothing, but some look worn out, with grey roots showing at the parting of their hair, not a scrap of makeup on, nor even a smile. I wonder what happened to them; why so tired?

I get off the bus and walk towards the precinct where the bank is located. Look through the stream of windows, individually placed like dominos on the line of terraced houses. I like to have a *nosey* at the different window settings. Some windows are dressed with blinds; or lined curtains, tied back so they look neat and tidy. Some curtains are still closed. A big, fat, ginger cat attracts my attention as it sits on the windowsill, licking away at its paws.

'Ahhh,' I say to myself, as I admire the simplicity of its life. I wish I was that cat today.

Something is distracting my eye away from the cat, a movement, just behind where the cat is sitting ... a wafting movement in the background snaps me out of my stare. I swiftly look away when I make eye contact with some poor soul minding their own business and watching the television in their own home. I hate it when that happens; the last thing they want is me peering through their window at this hour of the morning. It was a large figure in the background, a lady sat in her dressing gown, with 'just got out of bed' hair and a cigarette in her mouth.

I quicken my pace to get off the street and cross the road to walk towards the precinct. Look down at my shoes to make sure they look polished. I was once told that you can tell a lot about a woman if you look at her shoes, so I always make the effort.

I wonder if Jenny's in today, she's worked at this branch for a few years now. We meet up from time to time when we're sent on a development program. She's tall, with long, bouncy, shoulder-length, brown hair; you know the type, *'Because you're worth it'*. No doubt she'll be in her element at the moment because she's acting as branch manager, because her manager, Pam, is on maternity leave. I've never met Pam, but Jenny never has a good word to say about her. She always has a moan; I get the impression Jenny thinks she's better than everyone she works with.

My nose feels ice-cold. I cup my hand over it, blowing hot air; trying to create an airtight cup of heat. I feel relieved as I walk across the precinct and towards the door of the bank.

'Hi Lucy,' says Jenny, as I walk through the door and practically bump into her.

'Hi Jenny, how's things?'

'Fine, but you're early; shall we go for a coffee?'

'Sure, I've got half an hour.' We head out to the nearby coffee shop. I look at Jenny as we walk across the precinct. She seems distracted and I can see the strain in her face, as if she desperately needs to get something off her chest. I open the door of the coffee shop and we walk towards the counter.

'Come on,' I say, as we stand at the counter, waiting to be served.

'Okay, I do have something to tell you,' she says, looking surprised that I knew she was distracted. I order and pay for our coffees, watching the woman prepare our drinks. Coffee machines in these upmarket coffee shops amuse me, they look and sound like something from a spaceship. Huge, steel contraptions that spit, hiss and splatter as coffee vomits out of the metal tap when the waitress pulls a small lever downwards. We pick up our coffees from the counter and walk towards a table in the corner. Feeling relieved that the place is quite empty at this time of the morning; exhale as we place our cups onto the table and remove our coats.

'Come on then,' I prompt, not taking my eyes off hers as I blow on my coffee, trying to cool it down.

'Well, you know how my boss has been trying to promote me within work. And you know how Rick is so disorganised don't you,' she says, waiting for my reaction.

'He's not that bad!' I defend my own manager, as I study her eyes in case I miss something if I look away.

'I might be getting my first job as branch manager at your branch,' she announces, looking around to make sure no one can hear our conversation.

'You are!' I exclaim with alarm bells ringing in my head, negative alarms for sure!

'Rick will be okay, he's actually a good branch manager; the word out there is that he's got too comfortable at your branch. He is a better manager than me to be honest, so they want him to work in the main, city branch in Liverpool. Sales are down and everyone thinks Rick is the man to sort it. They reckon it'll be the firework up the backside he needs,' she says, as she sips her coffee. 'I wouldn't want our friendship to get in the way,' she continues.

'I'm sure you'll be fine!' I assure. Again, thinking to myself that we are not actual friends; I don't know where that came from. And I quite like working for Rick, yes, he's a bit disorganised, but that gives the rest of us a bit of freedom to develop and grow and have a laugh. I can't help but feel slightly disappointed.

'Great, but don't tell anyone. Rick doesn't even know yet,' she says quietly, as people start to arrive and sit around us.

'What if he doesn't want the city job?' I ask.

'Of course he will! It's a promotion. He'll be relieved he's not being sacked. He's totally lost his way, and the Regional Manager says he's seen it before. His fire has gone; he's not being challenged.'

'How do you know all this?'

'I've been managing our branch since Pam's been on maternity leave. She's due back in a couple of weeks, so they don't want me to go back to my previous role. I've been in all kinds of meetings. But I don't want you to think I've been unprofessional by telling you this.'

'Of course not, anyway, we'd best get back, I don't want the others at the branch thinking I'm brown-nosing with the branch manager!'

'Don't be daft; they know we're friends. I won't see you for the rest of the day anyway.'

Jenny said the word *friends* with a hint of insecurity in her voice, which isn't like Jenny; well, not from what I've experienced when we've been on a development program. I wonder if she has been swept along with the promotional thing in work, not wanting to feel as if she can't cope or do anything that she is being asked to do. When I last saw her, she seemed in control and confident. There seems to be a definite sheen of insecurity across her face, but I can't quite put my finger on it. Oh well, look at me *analysing* as usual.

As we arrive back at the branch, there's a buzz about the place.

'Has somebody won the lottery?' Jenny asks.

'No, we've all received an email about a competition for writing an advertising campaign for Insurance. The winner gets a prize of £2,000!' Michelle announces, sitting behind the reception desk.

'You'll be alright Lucy, seeing as you support the review of customer communications,' Jenny nudges.

'Well, you've made that sound more interesting than it actually is; I don't have anything to do with producing the material.'

'Well now's your chance,' Jenny says, as she steps into her office.

'Can you print off your email Michelle, I can never log into my mailbox in another branch,' I ask. Michelle seems alright, though I've only met her once before. She attended one development program, but Jenny treated her as if she was her PA. Jenny said she wasn't ready for development. I found that bizarre to be honest, but as usual the alarm bell would ring and disappear without me giving it a second thought. Michelle must be in her mid-20's. Gleaming, bleached-blonde, straight hair that gently flows against her back, midway between her shoulders and waist. Large, illuminated, blue eyes, decorated with thick, black, false eyelashes. I can't help but think she deserves to work somewhere better than here, but she seems happy enough.

'Here you go, you can have this one,' she says, with a smile, as she hands me a copy. I read the email as I log into a workstation, realising I still have my coat on.

'Lucy, you can put your bag in my locker; give me your coat too,' Jenny shouts, as she walks out of her office. She must have read my mind!

The day whizzes by and the change was nice. I'd soon get fed up after a week though. I definitely do need a complete change of direction in my life.

'I'll give you a lift home,' Jenny says, as she hands me my coat and bag at the end of the day.

'Great!' I say, as I put on the coat. I sit and relax in the reception area waiting for Jenny to finish off and lock up.

Sigh and melt into the chair as I take myself back to the first island in the swamp. Bitterly cold, frozen to my core, senses filled with a deep darkness, clouded thoughts. It feels like I'm being sucked out of work and forced to sit here ... alone.

There's no sign of Mike; he must have managed to scrape himself up and go to work. I really don't know how he does it, but he seems to manage his life better when he's getting drunk every night.

Dampness of the air melts into my face ... the only light is from the glow of the moon, transfixed in the sky like a torch low on battery. Its sorry-looking face is beaming down at me, trying to give me a bit of hope. I can't bring myself to smile. I don't feel as if I have anything to smile about; just feel dazed and confused. Swamp water has risen and started to *swallow* the surface of the island; it's shrunk in size. I pull my feet up and wrap my arms around my legs, leaning against the trunk of the tree. The strength of the trunk is the only support I have in my life. But even that isn't as solid as it was; I can hear crackling from inside ... it is slowly breaking down.

Distracted by snapping noises, cracking in a rhythm above my head, I'm shocked to see most of the branches have snapped off. Feeling so cold ... the jungle branches used to be strong, and feel as soft as leather, as they hung down towards the island. Protect me and make me feel safe ... but there's nothing I can do about it. I don't know what to do about it.

But I know I'm starting to become exposed ... my secret life is going to reveal itself.

'Come on then Lucy,' Jenny snaps, stood waiting to set the alarm at the door.

'Sorry Jenny, I was miles away then,' I say, as I get up off the chair and walk towards the door.

We walk behind the bank to where Jenny has parked her gleaming car. I open the passenger door and sit in the plush, black, leather seat and put on my seatbelt.

'Well, I bet you've already started to make notes about this advertising competition, haven't you?' Jenny asks.

'I have. Things like this always get me excited. I'll definitely give it a go.'

'You've always been good at writing and coming up with ideas; that's why I like being teamed up with you when we have to go on the development programs.'

'Thanks Jenny.'

'We'll get together if you want, after my holiday and I'll have a read of your material for the advertisement campaign,' Jenny says, as she checks her lipstick in the mirror.

We don't talk as Jenny reverses out of the parking space and revs the engine before roaring down the street to take me home. I can't think of anything to say as we only talk about work. That's how I know she's not a friend.

'Thanks Jenny, enjoy your holiday,' I say, as we pull up outside my house. Sigh, as I unbuckle my seat belt and step out of the car.

'See you Lucy,' she says, and as I shut the door, she once again checks her lipstick in the mirror and waves goodbye.

Walk down my path towards the front door, completely burdened, wading through the thickness of the swamp water. Heavy legs sink deeper; desperately cling onto branches as I drag myself to the second island.

But the fragile tree branches within the swamp waters are snapping as I grip. Falling, losing myself beneath the putrid water ... trying to get back to the surface; frantically feeling around for another stronger branch. Grabbing, clinging as I pull myself out from the water, praying it won't snap.

The strong wind feels completely exhausting as it pushes itself against my body. I can hear the creaking from within the branch as it moves in the wind. I hold onto it with all of my might and take a deep breath before I stretch out my arm to get hold of the next, and wade forwards. I don't feel strong enough to cope with this journey.

Aching arms, struggling to hold the weight of my body against the pull of the swamp water. The face of the moon is filtering away behind the jungle trees. It is frowning at me now with its hazy, bluish glow. The swamp water seems to be rising upwards towards my neck. Or, maybe I'm sinking, falling ... constantly slipping down, the branches near the second island have a slimy layer and it's difficult to keep hold.

Standing at my door, waiting to be hung, a heavy heart fills me with dread, drowning, suffocating. Staring at the key as I grapple with it in my right hand ... brute force suddenly flings back the door. Jolt backwards as I look up at Mike ... he likes me to see his sheer strength and authority, demonstrates it as clearly as a peacock extravagantly opening its elongated feathers.

'I was wondering who was in the car. It's nice to have you home at a normal time,' he says, as he hugs me.

'Mmm. Is John in?' I ask.

'No, he's out.'

I wish I had more time for my son John, but he doesn't need me as much now; he's 16 years old and has his own life. Work does seem to be overtaking though, I need to sort it. When I actually sit down and work out how many hours I work, I'm shocked to see that I actually work fifty-five hours a week, and not forty. No wonder I'm finding it hard trying to fit everything in. No wonder it feels like I'm in prison. But one thing I have to ask myself is why I'm working these hours. No one is physically forcing me to work them.

Even though I find myself feeling weighed down, I focus on the competition; a switch has been turned on. 'An Easy Guide to your Insurance Needs,' sounds simple, but blocking life out is what I'm doing; focusing on writing is just a distraction. It isn't going to make anything go away; I still have to deal with it all. But I don't know *how* to. Detachment is a life-saving tool, but I'm completely detaching myself without finding a solution; so that can't be good.

* * *

Fake smile plastered onto my dry, ashen face, slumped into my prison chair; the days are turning into weeks and there's no real change in my meaningless life. The competition has not brought me back to life. If anything, it's making my time here feel even more claustrophobic. I need to snap out of it! But these days, the only good time I have is when Melanie and I meet up each day for lunch. To amuse ourselves, we've started to *people watch*; our one-mile walks have become boring. Sitting and watching people as they walk or stumble by, we've witnessed domestic arguments, a day-time drunk with skid-marks on the *outside* of his trousers, frustrated mothers shouting at their kids ... the list goes on.

We noticed my manager Rick and his friend Andy meeting every day; we must be bored or desperate, or both! Andy owns the very unimaginatively-titled *Andy's Sandwich Bar*. There's no problem with the Rick and Andy meeting thing, it's just that Rick is married, with a young child and his beautiful wife is six months pregnant with their second. I'm sure he wouldn't do anything to jeopardise that. Melanie is so sure they're up to something ... I think she's wrong.

We're sat at the other end of the High Street on the empty benches where no one wants to sit any more. When the High Street was bustling, you couldn't get near them as they're near to the entrance to the gardens. The gardens form part of the main park and playing field that separates the High Street from the housing estate over the other side. The metal gates show signs of their previous beauty and magnificence. They are adorned with extravagantly scrolled, muscular-shaped, metal swirls. Practically go unnoticed these days; rusted, unloved, graffiti-adorned, flaking paint. People sometimes cut through the large playing field to get to the shops from the housing estate. If you follow the path to the left, it winds around and splits off into four separate little gardens; but no one bothers with them anymore, and everything's overgrown;

a complete mess. The path to the right leads to the playing field.

'Here's Rick and Andy again!'

'Oh yeah ... I don't even know why we're so fascinated by them,' I say.

'I told you, its Andy's hair and *transformation*; something's going on,' Melanie says, as she sits and stares. Rick and Andy giggle as they walk towards the entrance of the gardens.

Melanie's face is a picture, she's completely amused. Yes, there's been a bit of a *transformation*; he's changed his look, but don't we all at some time in our lives? He used to have jet-black hair that matched his jet-black eyebrows, which are pierced; but he's gone bleached blonde.

Andy was quite shy, but lately he is lavish and brash and showcases his new piercings. But you know, that is allowed, and doesn't mean there's a ridiculous reason behind it all …

'What the ...!' Melanie shrieks.

'What now?'

'Andy just grabbed hold of Rick's waist and pulled him close, that's what.'

'No!' I look at Melanie.

'Honestly, he did. Why would I even say anything like that; what would Vicky say?'

'Stop it Melanie, you must be mistaken.'

We both know Rick's wife, Victoria. Not Vicky, it's Victoria. She was always Vicky at school, so not sure what happened there. Maybe it's because she's the wife of a bank manager now!

'I am *not* mistaken; come on let's go and find out,' Melanie says, as she gets up from the bench.

'No, Melanie, I'm alright here!'

I don't even know why Rick takes the risk of meeting Andy each day. He must realise that people know him; he *is* the bank manager after all; and why walk down the High Street? Why not go out in his car and out of town?

'Come on Lucy, let's live dangerously for once. We need to take this project one step further,' she pleads, as she sits down with a look of encouragement on her face.

'Project? What project?' I ask.

'Project Sandwich!' We just need to find out which type of sandwich this is. Is it a spicy meatball and sausage sandwich? Or is it a plain old BLT?' she replies.

'When did Bacon, Lettuce and Tomato come into this?' I ask.

'Not that BLT, the ''Bloody hell Lucy, we are a pair of Tits.' You do know that this could all be in our minds and be innocent. Andy may be helping Rick with something. Maybe they're working on a surprise for Lady Victoria and the arrival of the new Prince or Princess,' she says, with a laugh.

'In *our* minds? I think it's just in *yours* Melanie!'

'At least it's brought a bit of excitement to our lunchtimes, hey Lucy?'

'Excuse me love.'

We both look up to see an unshaven workman standing in front of us. He has a high-vis waistcoat on over his jacket, and he's wearing scruffy jeans which are covered in dried paint.

'Today …' he says, in a tired voice. His face is expressionless; he's looking *through* us rather than *at* us.

'I need to ask you to move, so that we can tidy up this place.'

There's a large, white van parked further up next to the entrance of the gardens. The rear doors are open and there's another three workmen hanging around. We realise that this is it, it's today or never. Rick and Andy would definitely spot us if we sat here tomorrow. The four men with the high-vis waistcoats on are not really breaking into a sweat. It's an all-day job for them. And here's number five with the chip shop order in the carrier bags, one in each hand. Why five men to trim a few bushes?

'Today would be good,' the workman repeats.

Amused, Melanie stands up; she's got her way! Clasps my sleeve and tugs me away towards the van. I can't help but smile as she looks at her watch and then does some sort of sign language, prompting us to walk towards the gardens. I can't help but look up at the arched, metalled frame, an entrance to slumber in this dank place. And there's no sign of Andy and Rick. I'm relieved; I can breathe. The brisk wind is quite refreshing; I didn't feel it before.

'We should split up,' Melanie says, and she's quite serious too.

'No chance, not even in broad daylight; you don't know who's hanging around,' I say, just as seriously.

'Okay, well I'm not giving up yet; let's walk towards the gardens; they're overgrown and make an ideal hiding place.'

'They may have gone to Andy's house or something?' I say, half-hoping she'll agree and forget about this silly Project BLT.

'Come on Lucy; don't give up on me now. You may find something you can use to write about? Come on!'

'God knows what you think we're going to find,' I say, clinging onto her arm.

The air around us loses its light as we walk down the sheltered pathway amongst overgrown trees and bushes;

cocooned into darkness as we follow the dusty, dirt path, littered with broken foliage and dampened soil.

'The council will probably move into here and clear it, so Andy and Rick will have to find a new place to play,' she says.

'What goes on in that head of yours?' I sigh.

'We'll have to stay off the path; come on we'll walk behind these bushes.' Melanie pulls me off the path and onto the dampness of the soiled, overgrown, grass verges. I look down as we walk; my stilettos are like darts, collecting leaves and building up soil around my heel, changing the shape of my shoe. I have a block heel of soil.

'Shush! Keep quiet! Slow your pace too! We've got to be as quiet as possible,' Melanie whispers.

Echoed silence, a surreal moment as if I'm going to wake up from a bad dream, feeling for a reality as I step, and sink deeper into the moisture that has settled amongst the long grass and fallen foliage. The only clarity is the rustle within the surrounding bushes as we disturb the local wildlife.

'Get hold of the railing and squeeze around this bush,' she continues, as she crouches down to duck under a large branch that is sticking out at chest height.

'You've got to be kidding Melanie,' I whisper.

'Are you okay love?' a loud voice shouts.

We both look up from our crouched position and are faced with two smoking, bemused workmen on the other side of the railings.

'We're fine; can you keep your voices down. My cat's gone missing and a neighbour said they're sure they've seen it in here. But no doubt now after hearing your voice, it's run a mile,' she hisses.

'Sorry love, only trying to help,' he moans, as they walk away.

We stand up and I feel a bit embarrassed. I look at Melanie; she's got that brazen and determined look on her face, as usual.

'Let's just go for a walk, I think we're being silly now,' I say.

'You're probably right Lucy; come on we'll sit in one of the gardens, I've not been in here for a few years.'

Clamber back onto the encased pathway that leads to the gardens. Overgrown, billowing trees have formed a thick canopy overhead, which prevents daylight from filtering through and touching the ground or even the air around us. Walking through a dark tunnel as the pathway narrows and feels slimy underfoot; rotted foliage gelled into a carpet of furry, green moss.

'This used to be quite nice a few years ago; no doubt cutbacks are to blame,' Melanie sighs.

'I know, but at least we're getting to do a bit of a walk today though. But you do know that if we scream for help, there's no way those workmen are going to come to our rescue.'

'This is a hellhole. Let's hope they're starting in here today; it doesn't feel safe, does it?' Melanie replies.

'You're getting me worried now, let's turn back.'

'Got ya!' Melanie hisses, as she pulls me behind a bush on the left side of the path. 'I forgot about that,' she continues.

'What?' I whisper.

'That old sandwich van over there.'

I peep over the edge of the bush, and I see a dilapidated, rectangular van. It's obviously not been used for years.

'Andy used to run his sandwich business from a van; *that* sandwich van over there. He used to have a spot just out of town on the trading estate. But he opened his shop on the High Street about four years ago, and never bothered with it after that. He used to have a young lad working for him, and then the council agreed to let him trade from the van, in these gardens. He'd open it up when the car boot sales were on each week, or a Gala and Bonfire night. But that all stopped about three years ago,' Melanie says.

'I can't remember.'

'Memory like a sieve, you have. We used to call him the *entrepreneur* of the High Street. Come to think of it, a few months ago, that nosey cow at my place said that Andy had been served with a notice to remove the van. Otherwise, if the council were forced to move it, they'd charge him for it. I just didn't take much notice at the time,' Melanie continues. 'State of it; it's a health hazard!'

Taking a closer look, I can see that the wooded area has tried to envelop the van. Ivy has wrapped itself across the roof and down the whole of one side. Green moss and seasonal dirt has tried to camouflage it. The surrounding, overgrown bushes and lack of light have kept it hidden from view. Who in their right mind would come here anyway?

'We've come this far; I'm going in,' Melanie says, and begins to move forward.

'Wait a minute! What do we do if they are in the van?' I whisper.

'I'll say that I offered to take a look at the van, because Paul's got the job of removing it,' Melanie says, as I pull her back. 'I'll also have a go and say that I didn't realise how dangerous it was, and if he'd had the decency to get it moved when the council asked, I wouldn't be in this position,' Melanie announces. She's got it covered!

I can't believe I'm here; no doubt it is BLT and it'll be empty. It'll probably collapse on top of us and serve us right if it does. I can just make out the faint red wording *Andy's*, over the boarded-up serving hatch. We creep towards it; my skin feels cold against the dampness of the air; uncomfortable in this sickly atmosphere.

Deathly silent, a hazy fog released within our deep, slow breaths. Half-hidden behind brazen Melanie, I press myself against the side of the van. I look out towards the tunnel of darkness. The dirt path leading to the tunnel is strewn with wet leaves. The dampened soil is slimy and swamp-like in places; the tunnel has a darkened circle as its entrance door. Light is desperately trying to reach inside it from above and I can see lightness in the distance as I look right into the centre. It's then I realise we've just stepped out of that tunnel, and we're completely shut off from the outside world. I feel a little nervous. The natural tunnel has led us into this open space, but it's still very overgrown with no real sunlight reaching us. The trees are very tall in this part of the gardens, so the air is a little lighter, but they're still acting as an overhead screen. Melanie pulls me closer towards her ... she's too impatient sometimes.

'Owww,' I say, as I stumble over the tow bar that's attached to the van.

'Sorry!' Melanie's voice whispers through the air as she looks down at me lying on the floor.

As I lie here, frantically rubbing my sore leg, I can hear something from inside the van; a sort of groaning. I put my hand over my mouth; one false move and we're caught out. Surely this can't be a Spicy Meatball and Sausage sandwich? Not Rick?

I can't look at Melanie; I'll either laugh or scream and run. I can feel that Melanie is moving away from me. She is shimmying around to the rear of the van. I pick myself up off the floor and peer towards her; watching as she slowly moves. As she furtively creeps along the back of the van, moss is attaching itself to her coat. She reaches the doorway; I crouch down and move towards her. I can see that she is trying to find a spy hole, to find out what is going on inside. Is this legal? Don't 'pervs' do this sort of thing? I hold my breath as Melanie reaches for the door handle; I can't believe it as I watch what she is doing. My heart is beating slowly and intensely, like a fluffy, bass-drum beater hitting a large drum; as dramatic as watching a symphonic orchestra. Waiting with bated breath each time the beater muffles against the drum. Melanie was never one for handling delicate situations. I move towards her in a dazed, zombie-like state. My hand is over my mouth as she slowly pulls the handle down. I can see the sheer concentration in her face; I no longer exist to her. It feels as if this moment has suddenly gone from slow-motion to fast-forward and chaotic, as she swings open the door with brute force. The top hinge of the door is broken, so it's only held on by the bottom hinge. The door is obviously heavy because it completely falls off, and nearly lands on top of me. I jump out of the way and land with a thud on the floor. Melanie hasn't seen that though, and doesn't care; no, she's going in there.

The sudden commotion is immense. I'm sat amongst the leaves, and they feel quite damp; probably because they don't get one drop of sun at the back of this van. My hands squelch into the dampness of the soggy grass and leaves.

'I hope you wash your hands before you go back and make sandwiches?' Melanie shouts, from within the van. 'It's not every day you see a sandwich maker with their pants down. Your business would go down too if people knew what I found today. And as for you ... how's Vicky?'

She's purposely used the shortened form Vicky to aggravate Rick. I sit helplessly as he comes flying out of the van. He stops for a second to look down at me. I'm still sat, with both hands squelched into the ground, holding myself up, and my legs are stretched out amongst the leaves. He doesn't say anything, not even a 'hello'. He's looking right through me as if he's searching for my soul. I sit open-mouthed as he zips up his trousers and walks away towards the tunnel. Melanie steps out of the van looking quite pleased with herself. She actually remembers that I'm with her and holds out her hand to help me up.

'Don't worry, my hands are clean,' she sniggers, as she pulls me up.

'Make sure you move the van within the next week; the council are waiting to clean up this mess!'

'That's enough,' I shout, as I watch Andy walk quickly away from the van towards the tunnel.

'Lucy, your coat's filthy; it's full of moss,' Melanie says, as she tries to rub it off.

'Yours is the same.'

'I'm not going back out onto the High Street looking like this!'

'I'm off this afternoon anyway, I forgot to tell you. Why don't you ring in sick and come to mine; you can get cleaned up,' Melanie offers.

'I'll have to. I might lose my job,' I say, exhausted.

'Will you heck! Rick will be panicking now, you may even get promoted.'

'I'll ring work when I get back to yours. He should keep it out of town if he's playing away,' I add.

Melanie and I take off our coats and carry them across our arms as we walk to her house. We link arms as we walk towards the dark tunnel. My ruined shoes squelch further into the dampness of the ground, sinking deeper into the muddy consistency as I take each step. Struggling to move forward, impatient Melanie lets go of my arm and powers ahead; causing me to lose sight of her. Falling to the ground, desperately trying to pull my legs out of the mud, I manage to scramble upwards onto harder ground, finally reaching the entrance of the tunnel.

Slowly inch myself forward as I feel my hands in front of my body. Pitch-black, the tunnel feels more enclosed and claustrophobic. Feeling scared, my hands touch a cold, hard surface and it stops me in my tracks. Frantic, panicking pressure as I push myself against the solid surface. But my feet keep sliding backwards and there's no movement in the solidity. Feel around and the solidity reaches from the ground and up to the top of the tunnel. Slowly turn as a noise from behind disturbs me. Frozen stiff, I feel breathless, as a dark figure pulls itself out of the mud that lies near to the entrance of the tunnel. Misshapen, but familiar, a faceless creature, stood motionless. A dreaded, atmospheric silence as my focus remains on this being. Startled, jump out of my skin as the figure suddenly starts pounding towards me as it enters the tunnel.

'Help, I need help!' I scream, as I hit the hard surface, frantically feeling for a way out. In my absolute panic I feel a door handle and push it downwards. Throw myself through and close the door behind me, desperately trying to prevent whatever it is on the other side from getting through. Slump to the ground, leaning against the door, as the power of Fear desperately tries to reach me.

The force from the other side suddenly stops, and it's then I realise I'm sat on the second island in the swamp. Suffocated by the jungle heat, I feel tightness around my neck. Not sure if it's dehydration, or whether I've come to the end of the road with it all. I can't see any sign of Mike; I'm not sure if he's in my world today, or whether I'm actually still managing to completely block him out of mine. I'm sure I can hear Melanie's loud voice from over the other side of the jungle trees. That's the first real sound that I've heard here. Maybe I'm starting to let people back into my life again, now that I'm out of that field. I never felt lonely in there though, even though I was alone. I feel more alone than ever now. I've got to finally listen to myself and sort things out.

'Earth to Lucy! Earth to Lucy!' I faintly hear Melanie say.

'Sorry Melanie, was I miles away again?'

'You've been in a world of your own. Where do you go to sometimes? I know today's been a bit of a shock and it's my fault, but at least you never actually witnessed anything. Come on, pull yourself together. I'll get the kettle on,' she laughs. We've arrived at Melanie's house already; she's right, I do go off sometimes. I don't even remember getting here; probably a good job Melanie was linking my arm.

'Do you want a shower?' Melanie asks.

'I think I'll have to. I'll have to borrow a pair of trousers or something from you too,' I say, as I check out my muddy knees and backside.

'No problem, I put a load of clean washing on my bed this morning; there's a couple of pairs of jogging bottoms. Get a pair on and throw your trousers down. I'll get them in the wash with your coat,' Melanie says, as she takes my coat out of my hands.

In the upstairs bathroom, I look at myself in the mirror.

'I look so old and haggard,' I say to myself. 'What's happened to you Lucy? You need to get yourself together; remember *you*, the one who was always laughing; the one who was always positive and never let anything get you down?'

I think my life sort of went downhill when Mike moved in, but that may just be coincidence; I've just got to figure it out. I'm certainly not going to figure it out now in Melanie's bathroom, so I take off my dirty clothes and wrap a large towel around my body. I turn on the shower and walk out of the bathroom.

'Here you go Melanie,' I shout, as I throw my dirty trousers down the stairs. I walk back into the bathroom for a refreshing shower.

'You don't have milk or sugar in your coffee, do you?' Melanie shouts.

'Just strong and black for me,' I shout back, sitting on the side of the bath, drying myself down.

I look out across to the third island ... tall trees grow out from the swamp water to the left of it. They are encasing that side of the island, and it is slightly out of view from where I'm sitting. The trees are dark-brown and leaves only grow from the top; they don't hang down towards the island. The trees to the right of the island are deep green in colour and there is a lot of foliage and greenery growing out of the water. The leaves and branches look fur-lined and soft, and definitely wouldn't hold my weight. The centre of the island is shining in a honey, golden glow. The sun must be raining down from an opening above; and the backdrop of trees have strong branches hanging down towards the island like large drapes. The glow looks warm and inviting, but there are no jungle trees in between this island and the next. I'm not sure how I'd make my way there with no branches to hold onto.

I pull on a pair of jogging bottoms and t-shirt and place the damp towel in the washing basket. Sigh, as I walk downstairs and into the living room. Melanie is sat on the settee.

'You certainly broke our cover didn't you,' I accuse Melanie, as I sit down next to her.

'I couldn't help it. When I realised what was going on, it made me angry and I had to confront it immediately,' she says, and sits in thought for a moment. 'It's not the gay side; I don't care about that at all. It's the unfaithful side of things. It happened to me didn't it,' she sighs.

'That did you a favour though because you've got a great husband now. Don't dwell on that and don't feel you have to make excuses for what happened. Rick and Andy put themselves in that position, and to be honest we've done them a favour.'

'How do you figure that out?'

'They may not have known that the workmen were about to embark on the clear-up. They may have been inside when the workmen arrived. In fact, if Rick confronts me, I'll tell him. He's lucky we found them.'

'You're right,' Melanie says, as she sips her coffee. 'It was fate; fate *saved* them,' she adds.

'I'd best ring work,' I say, as I take my phone out of my bag; it's buzzing.

'Hello.'

'Lucy,' a male voice says.

'Yes.'

'It's Rick from work.'

'Oh, hello Rick, I was just going to ring you. I didn't feel well this morning and I got worse at lunch. I was ringing to say I won't be coming back this afternoon, but I'll be back in the morning.'

'I need to talk to you.'

'If it's about today, don't worry, I won't say anything, and I just need to get over the shock of it. I'll be okay tomorrow, I'll speak to you then,' I say, and end the call.

'He's got a nerve,' Melanie says.

'Don't ... not today. I just want to chill,' I plead, not wanting any more drama.

'That wash will be done now; it's only a quick 30-minute one. I'll peg our stuff out and it'll be dry in about three hours. You might as well crash here for the afternoon. Won't be a minute.'

Vibrating hand as my phone buzzes ... I don't want to answer it, but begrudgingly I do.

'Hello.'

'Hi Lucy, it's Jenny. I'm back from my hols now, so I'll try and get together with you to look at what you've written for the competition.'

'Thanks Jenny. But only if you have the time.'

'I'm busy getting ready for the branch manager role, but I'll do my best. See you soon.'

A part of me doesn't want Jenny to look at my work. Something isn't feeling right, but as usual the alarm bell rings in my head and then disappears without a second thought. As soon as Jenny gets to our branch, I need to have a chat. I don't want to work extra hours, reviewing customer communications anymore. I'm not working the two late evenings, and half-day Saturday anymore either.

Closed eyes and relaxed mind, as the warmth from the gleaming sun sweeps between the jungle trees on the third island and across the waters to where I'm slumped. I really want to get to the other side of those trees. A comfortable warmth as my heart fills with hope and a real smile rises within me.

'What are you smiling about?' Melanie asks, as she passes me a piece of cake.

'I feel human today, doing silly things with you.'

'You need a week or two off, you do; you're not yourself. You don't open up like you used to do,' she says.

I know she's right, but I don't say anything out loud. I think it in my head. I have gone into myself because I'm thinking too much lately. I need to get control of my life ... I've just got to figure out how to do it.

Chapter 3

'Is Rick in today?' I ask, as I stumble into work and glimpse Carol, slumped in her chair at the reception desk. No 'happy to help' smile or motion.

'No, he's on holiday. He's sent us all an email,' she sighs, without lifting her head. 'There you go, here's a copy; it's a riveting read!' she announces, as she waves a printed copy in front of my face.

Checking the time; no time to stop and chat. I take it out of her hand and input the numeric security code to open the door that leads to the stairs. Sigh, as I walk up the stairs and enter the dark, empty locker room. Feeling disappointed, as my life is these days, I shove my coat and bag into the miniscule locker. Deep, slow, controlled breathing as I try to calm the panic inside. Thumping heartbeat, in tune with every heaving step I take, walking down the stairs and back through the door into the reception area. Blinded by the intensifying sun as it blazes through from the High Street; step into the shade and gaze outside towards the two red-brick, domineering buildings on the opposite side of the street. The sun towers over them and stretches its glare directly onto the cobbled alleyway that runs between, then across the street and into the reception area inside the bank. Overpowering structures of character, the 'King and Queen' of the High Street; looking down their noses at the lack of architecture in the newer buildings. Beautiful, original, leaded windows surrounded by sculptured sand-stone and deep-red brick.

'Have you read it yet?' Carol asks, still not looking up from whatever she's doing.

'No, I'll read it now.'

'Sit on these chairs and read it, I want to know what you think!' she murmurs, elbows pointing and balancing on the desktop. An expressionless face cupped into both hands. Looking tired and peaky; a dry complexion and unsightly, dark rings around her wrinkled, dark-brown eyes. Like the before picture on *10 years younger* ... a study of her face gives me a glimpse of what she would look like if she was made over. Slightly curled, long eyelashes would look amazing if she bothered to wear make-up. Concealed eyes and a touch of lipstick on those near-invisible lips would bring her back to life ... like the first breath when receiving lifesaving, mouth-to-mouth resuscitation.

Empty chairs, lined against the wall next to the reception desk. Charcoal-grey, padded seating; pure-black, metal legs.

Hand brushes against the rough material as I pull one away from the wall and sit down.

'Well?' Carol asks.

'I'm reading it now.'

> *Hello everyone*
> *Sorry I couldn't tell you in person but I'm on holiday for the next few days; then, as of next Monday I'm moving to one of our main branches in Liverpool.*
> *I've enjoyed working with you all, and sorry to go but I couldn't miss this opportunity. I'll be working on an urgent project, so I hope you all understand.*
> *You can still contact me by email if you need me for anything.*
> *Rick*

'Ha ha ha!'

'What are you laughing at?' asks Carol.

'Nothing really, it's just that it's the same everywhere, we're just an employee number. People move on I guess,' I sigh, feeling bewildered and perversely amused at the word *project*.

'I know what you mean; I wouldn't dream of just getting up and going like he has. All out for himself; his head was right up his own arse,' she says.

Force a smile, before I sigh, as I get up from the chair. Half of the sigh is for the relief of not having to face Rick and the other half is because I will actually miss him. He always believed in me and I sort of need that at the moment.

'Big Brother's on us already,' Carol shouts from the reception desk.

'What's wrong now?' I shout over as I sit at my workstation.

'Jenny's emailed us to say she starts next Monday! That's all we need, another *know-it-all*,' Carol sighs.

As I flick through my emails, I can see why Carol isn't best-pleased. Ultra-keen Jenny will want to make an impression. She's asking us to complete all kinds of questionnaires and forms. Every part of me is being analysed!

'She'll be taking urine samples before we know it,' Carol adds.

'I know what you mean,' I laugh.

Feeling stressed; I really don't want to be probed when Jenny gets here …

* * *

A fleeting, real smile as I break away from the drudge and turmoil of working life. Meeting Melanie for our usual lunch-time escape; fighting against the bleakness, as another High Street shop is emptied and boarded-up. Step onto damp slabs of dull-grey paving-stones; look into the distance as I catch sight of Melanie, and her determined stride.

'I fancy a sandwich today for lunch; I forgot to make something last night,' Melanie announces, smiling smugly.

'I thought we'd had enough of sandwiches!'

'I fancy trying Andy's,' Melanie smirks.

'Oh Melanie, can't we just move on from that, and find a new project?' I plead.

'Lucy, this is me you're talking to. Come on!'

I lag behind like a dog on a lead as we walk down the High Street. I feel exhausted as Melanie struts into 'Andy's'.

Step inside for the first time; an instant, homely feel; very cosy. Look around as determined Melanie taps her fingers on the counter, waiting to be served. Two small, round tables set out against the large window. Dark-mahogany, wooden tables, covered over with red and white, checked tablecloths. There are four mahogany wood, high-backed chairs, tucked underneath each table. They are set with red salt, vinegar and pepper pots; four placemats and knives and forks wrapped in red napkins. The centrepiece is a wax-encrusted, empty bottle of wine with an un-lit candle sticking out of the top. A black board is fixed to the main wall, with sandwich *specials* chalked onto it.

'No Andy today?' she asks.

I cheer up when I realise, he's not in.

'No, he's on holiday,' says a young lad, as he wipes the surface of the counter.

'That's a shame. I hear he does a marvellous meatball and spicy sausage sandwich!'

'We're out of meatballs,' the lad answers.

'I bet you are! And do you know if he's arranged to move that unsightly heap of a snack bar out of the gardens?'

Bewildered, I can't help but examine his youthful, under-reaction. Unfazed, can't-be-bothered attitude, as he tries to read Melanie with his lazy, tired, hazel-green eyes. The silence between them should be on today's specials board ... with a free, cutting service. I feel like I've been transformed into a judge witnessing a blinking competition. No expression within his long, narrow face or movement in his slight, gangly frame. Sudden movement snaps us out of our stare, as he runs his right hand through his chestnut-brown, shoulder-length, wavy hair. Soft, yet dull hair, that adds a bit of life to his bone structure.

'Who are you? Are you from the Council?' the lad questions.

'Yes, I am; when is Andy due back?' Melanie asks.

'I'm not sure. If that's all, I need to serve other customers today,' he continues.

'Let's hope for your sake I don't work with the Environmental Health Department; wear a hairnet for goodness sake!' Melanie sneers and turns to walk out.

Stepping back out onto the High Street, we suddenly stop in our tracks as we almost bump into Victoria.

'Hi Victoria, how are you doing?' I ask.

'I'm fine, I'll be glad when I get this pregnancy over with,' she says, as she opens her coat and shows us how big she's getting. 'I've only got a couple of months to go, so can't wait,' she continues. 'Anyway, I suppose you've heard about Rick's fantastic new job?' she gloats.

'We did hear,' I answer.

'Is your Paul still labouring and running around for the council?' Victoria asks Melanie, in a spiteful tone, which appals me.

'He is he's still clearing out hellholes. Which reminds me, hasn't Rick found himself inside a hellhole? Isn't that why he moved jobs?' Melanie asks.

Stood open-mouthed, too shocked to react, I wait in suspense to see how Victoria responds, but she doesn't know how to; she just storms off.

'Before you say anything,' Melanie says, but then I interrupt her.

'Victoria's attitude is a disgrace! No doubt she'll mention something to Rick though,' I sigh.

'Don't start worrying about him? Let's have a sit down and eat, come on, that bench is free.'

Look across at Melanie's tormented face as I feel the bench with my hands to check that it isn't damp. It's dry, but cold; press my coat against my legs as I sit down.

'She's always had it in for me; she's a right spoilt bitch. Don't ask me to go on any nights out with her again!' Melanie seethes.

'Don't worry, I won't be going on any; and anyway, Rick's moved on now.'

'I've just remembered I didn't get anything for lunch. I'll be back in a minute,' Melanie moans, as she walks off towards the shops.

Vibrations ... vibrating from within my handbag; rummage around for my mobile phone, pull it out and look at it, puzzled; not recognising the number that's flashing at me.

'Hello,' I answer.

113

'Lucy?'

'Yes.'

'It's Rick.'

'Oh.'

'I need to talk to you! Can we meet up sometime?'

'When and where?'

I'm not sure; I'm helping to judge the competition entries this week. Can I text you on Friday?'

'Okay,' I sigh. Rick and I were quite close in work; he was always pushing me to do more, always trying to increase my self-confidence; but you know, that's something I have to start doing myself.

'Thanks, and I am sorry. You didn't deserve that, no one does,' Rick says, and then ends the call.

'Who was that?' Melanie questions, as she sits next to me.

'Oh, that was Rick. He wants to meet me some time to talk.'

'You're not going to meet him, are you?'

'I have to, for my sake more than his. He sounded really down too.'

'Well, you're best keeping out of it; he got himself into this mess!' Melanie spits.

'I know, but Rick and I always worked well together.'

'I know, and no doubt you and Jenny will too. Just let me know what happens.'

'Will do,' I sigh.

Back at my workstation, reading emails and serving customers with a forced smile. Exhausted, and unfocused, I'm reading the emails two and three times, until the detail reaches my brain. Excited smile, as I read an email, inviting me to a ceremony in a posh hotel next Friday. The work I completed for the competition has been put forward for judgement!

* * *

It's Friday! Feeling confident and excited, sat in Jenny's sports car, as we make our way to the hotel.

'You look different,' Jenny asks, as she peeks over at me, trying to keep her eye on the road.

'I let myself go for a while, but I'm trying to get my life back on track,' I announce.

'How come you let yourself go? I noticed you had, but I didn't like to say. It's funny isn't it; everyone falls over themselves to tell us if we lose weight. But, if we dare to put it on, no one says anything to our faces; they just snigger behind our back!'

'Well, I won't even ask who's been sniggering.'

'I didn't mean you! I just meant in general.'

'I don't know what happened to me. I used to go the gym every day. I lost myself for a while, I guess.'

Jenny doesn't answer, as if she wants me to continue.

'I feel quite angry at myself, for letting myself go. I've got no self-confidence.'

'That's a bit deep isn't it,' Jenny says, as we pull up to the hotel.

A sudden silence between us as Jenny spies a senior executive from head-office, parking his car over the other side of the carpark. She quickly steps out of the car and speed-walks over. Amused, I step out of the car and walk towards the entrance of the hotel; got no time for brown-nosing. I feel a little uncomfortable now that I have confided in Jenny. She's totally swooning over the exec; no room for him to step out of his car even if he wanted to. She's stood at the driver's door, talking and giggling.

I walk into the spacious reception area. A free-standing noticeboard confirms directions to the conference suite. I walk along a narrow corridor which has doorways dotted along it on either side. A gold-plated sign with an arrow pointing to the right confirms where the suite is.

Smile, as I enter the room. There's a desk at the front with a projector shining a light on the wall behind it. A huge, oval-shaped table sits in the centre. The executives are sat at another table, at the back of the room. Refreshments have been laid out on a table, behind them. I hate that I have to walk past to get my usual coffee. I wouldn't mind if they made an effort to speak to us on a day-to-day basis, but for some unknown reason, they are unable to do so. I make every effort not to make eye contact as they'll never speak to me again. Rick walks into the room and immediately sees me too. I walk over; at least he's sort of normal.

'Hi.'

'Hi,' he says, looking a bit uncomfortable and embarrassed.

'How's Liverpool?' I ask, trying to ease the situation.

'It's great, I'm really enjoying it. It's like the missing piece of a jigsaw,' he says, with a big smile; a smile I've not seen for a long time but recognise from a few years ago.

His mesmerising smile captivates me as I glimpse his full, rose-coloured lips and perfect white teeth. Navy-blue eyes look incredible against his dark features and jet-black, designer-cut, cropped hair.

'That's great!'

'You should come with me,' Rick says.

'Come where?'

'Work in Liverpool with me! You *do* know that there will only be room for Jenny and no-one else at your branch now,' he continues.

Feeling puzzled, I don't know how to answer him.

'I didn't realise I needed to escape until I was forced,' he adds.

'I admit I'm fed up with my life, but I'm fed up of working all hours. If I work further away from home, I'll be away more,' I say.

'Not if the money was better. I could arrange it so you're working from home one day a week too,' Rick offers.

'I'll see,' I sigh. I don't want to take him too seriously, but then again, a part of me would love to go and work for him again. 'I'll catch up with you later,' I say, as I sit down. I need to get over Project Sandwich; maybe I'll be able to take him seriously then.

In a room with virtual strangers, I look around as Jenny's piercing, false laugh echoes down the corridor as she walks into the room with the senior executive. Eyes transfixed onto him, as she leads them both to the refreshments table. Exhausted, I don't want to make any effort today; I don't want to have to talk about *my* life because I don't know what *my* life is any more. Jenny's false, over-the-top laugh is as sharp and annoying as a sudden fire-alarm. Pouring coffees and plating up biscuits for them both; pass me the sick bucket now! She's totally brown-nosing her way to the top. So glad I never confided in her about Rick; she'd strike him down in a flash. Maybe I should think about Rick's offer, knowing why he wants me to work for him. He is a little disorganised, so I cover his back, do some of his work; it leaves room for us to breathe. A total control freak like Jenny will suffocate us. We'll all die in our chairs; I can feel my neck tightening as I think about it.

Tom, the facilitator, enters the room in a blaze of glory. Like a Rock God walking on stage in a cavernous concert arena.

'Hello team!' he bellows, as he bounces around demonstrating *air guitar*.

I don't believe it - he's mic'd up so that he energizes us all with his moves. He is slightly overweight and wearing a sky-blue, cotton shirt that must be one size too small. The buttons around his stomach are severely under pressure, the buttonholes are stretching out from behind the buttons. White flesh and dark, wiry hairs are making an appearance. He has thinning, light-ash, brown hair and a plaited, goatee beard. His face brightens the morning; very friendly, enlightened smile. His small, grey eyes and tiny mouth are unnoticeable until he smiles. The stench from his over-powering aftershave is knocking me sick as he tumbles around the room.

'Okay! Well, I've spent the last two days with your senior management team,' he announces, as he looks over at the executives' table.

I should have brought my autograph book.

'Shall we get the back table to introduce themselves?'

'Hello, I'm a well-worn table just minding my own business. I get cleaned regularly and rode on … on the rare occasion,' says a tiny voice from the back of my wandering mind.

'Okay, why don't you tell the room a bit about yourselves,' he excitedly asks the executives on the back table and passes one of them a mic.

Feeling selfishly ignorant, with no desire to hear what they have to say.

Treacherous rain; droplets feel as hard as hail-stone as they strike my body. Huddled against the weakened trunk, I feel like I'm being pelted from every direction. There's no shelter on this island, the jungle tree growing out from the centre is now very slight. Looking out towards the flourishing trees on the third island; they would definitely offer me the shelter I desperately need. A large, white heron forages on that island, it's the first time I've seen any kind of wildlife. I know I need to move from here, but I feel too weighed down to do anything. Consumed by self-pity, I feel more comfortable sitting here, allowing myself to be tortured by the jungle rain. The droplets are falling with intense speed, as if thousands of bullets are being shot downwards into the swamp water. And the force of them entering the swamp is causing the water to splash upwards; the surface looks like it has a layer of gravel on the top of it, like a gravelled pathway. And it's then I realise I do need to move forwards.

I just didn't realise that or see the detail when I was stuck in my field. Ignoring my surroundings. I know I wasn't looking through *my* eyes, though not sure whose eyes I've been looking through. I know I've not been *me* for a long time.

* * *

A day off work last week, I went out to the local shops in the next town; I hadn't been there for years. Standing still for a while, just watching as people busied past me, getting on with their daily lives. I was in slow-motion, they were on fast-forward. Turning around in the spot I was standing, in the middle of the busy pathway just off the High Street. Feeling confused but awake and aware of my surroundings; taking in the architecture of the buildings; hearing the noises I hadn't taken any notice of for years. I don't know how long I was stood there for. But I just walked away once I'd heard enough and went to my car. Yes, my car, the one I don't get to use much any more; even that's been taken away since Mike moved in. Sitting in the car in silence, for a while, not really thinking, gave me time to *see*. And when I got home I saw things for what they really were.

My house had become a drinking den. It was always pristine, fragranced; small, but perfectly formed. But not on that day; I actually saw it for real, as I shut the front door behind me. The stair-carpet looked worn-out and tatty. The rest of the house had already had carpets removed and replaced with laminate. Mike wasn't interested, but he wouldn't move out either. I always presumed it was because I worked too hard, but that's not true as there's still hours left in the day when I get home. Someone else had given me their eyes for a while; maybe I'll never find out whose. I don't want to die, but I'm not living either. I'm not sure what I'm doing. As I'm sat here, I feel a rage come over me. *There is a life inside of me.*

Warm embrace of the sun against my face, as it breaks out across the water, and into my slumber. Harsh rain no longer beating at me, as I stand to look out towards the honey-yellow glow beaming downwards onto the centre of the third island. Squelching feet pressed into the muddied surface;

contemplating how to move forward with no branches to ease my journey. Slippery underfoot, my feet are sinking; difficult to pull them back out; exhausting. Slip and slide downwards, frantically trying to stop myself against the slimy consistency. Freezing water takes my breath away, shockingly cold against my quivering body, the disgusting stench revolts within the disturbed, underlying filth.

A sudden, heavy weight on my back takes me in its complete grasp, forcing me under the swamp water, taking full control of my whole body. Writhing around in the water, struggling to get back up to the surface; desperately trying to shake myself free. I *want* to break free. My arms are tightly forced against each side of my body. A feeling of being strapped, imprisoned, trapped ... feeling hopeless, I realise its Mike; he doesn't want me to move forward with my life. He wants me to stay here with him.

'Fucking stop struggling now!' he storms.

'I don't want to. You're forcing me to live a life I don't want to live!'

'Get a grip you fucking idiot, no one else would want you anyway.'

'Leave me alone, get off me.'

Tugging on my shoulders, desperately trying to push me back under the water, he's using his full body weight to anchor me down. I'm desperately holding onto my soul, not going down with him; I've fallen low enough. I kick backwards but the drag of the swamp water prevents me from kicking with full force. There's nothing I can do but fall with him ... fall down below the swamp water as I lose my grip ... lose a grip on *my* life. I feel as if I'm free-falling ... feel as heavy as an anchor that's being launched into the sea from a ship. Falling to the bottom of the swamp-bed with such force and speed, there's nothing I can do. I can't breathe or see anything. All I know is that I've got Mike hanging onto me for dear life. He's hanging on to my last breath; completely drained me emotionally, physically and financially ... this is his last attempt at completely and utterly controlling everything about me. I can feel the putrid water enter my body. Mike has his heavy hand on my head as he forces me down with him. Crying and pleading with him ... I wish I was dead! Maybe I *have* died, and the realisation hasn't set in.

Landing with a thud at the bottom of the swamp, the shock brings me back to life and I open my eyes. Mike loses his balance and his grip on me, and topples over, falling flat on his back and he can't get up. I watch as an under-current tries to carry him away. He's grappling with the bed of the swamp, trying to cling onto anything, but he's being carried away from me and away from *my* space. Looking at me with those awful eyes of his; intimidating me to get *his* way ... to drain me ... he is a *life drainer*. I can see swirling sediments disturbed from the swamp-bed; Mike's clinging onto rocks, pulling them loose as he battles to stay; but he's being dragged away. The released pressure is creating spraying eruptions of small pebbles. I can sense his anger and desperation; desperate hands, grabbing, fiercely stretching to reach me, to punish me. Racing heart, exhausted, confused, overshadowing the relief I should be feeling as Mike disappears within murky, shadowed water. I don't have the energy to make my way back up to the surface, I want to stay here and drown ... But then I realise, he's always doing this to me ... he drags me down, drags me to a place he knows I won't move from. Then when he knows he's got me where he wants me, he'll do whatever he pleases; he won't be giving me a second thought.

I can stay here and drown; or I can find a way out of this life. And with that thought I can feel a change in the current ... it's dark and murky, but I can sense something surging towards me. With such intent, it completely freaks me inside out. I stand up, bend my legs and push myself up from the bed of the swamp. Feeling something behind me, grabbing for my feet ... completely petrified ... forcing myself upwards as putrid water continues to enter my body and tries to end my life. I'm frantically breathing the water inside of me; it's seeping through my entire body. A feeling of entering but not drowning as I move upwards; I'm forcing my hands and arms up as high as I can to get to the surface. Kick downwards at whatever is torturing me from below. My kick forces Fear away as I reach the surface of the swamp. Vomiting water and filth, I feel for a grip on the third island as I struggle to breathe. Pull myself upwards as I cling onto a jungle branch; drag myself onto the island and lie there, looking back towards the second. My exhausted body is frantic and empty.

Nothing left to give.

Half-open eyes; too exhausted to fully function. Punishing myself through a daily, excruciating routine, I can see Mike ranting and raving on the second island. He's destroying what's left of the jungle tree, punching holes into the trunk. Wanting to make his hands bleed as if he's actually punishing himself. Exhausted, cramped stomach; vomiting as I lie, curled up into the foetal position. Struggling to breathe and make sense of what's going on ... all I can do is lie and stare. Stare out at the chaos Mike's creating for himself and the rest of us. I feel robotic as I lie half-dead, trying my best to stay alive. Pure-white, shivering skin cloaked in thick mud from head to toe. My clothing is torn and worn out. Mike's grappling with the trunk of the jungle tree, shaking it, strangling the last bit of life out of it. I lie watching him in his manic tirade. The trunk practically explodes its contents out onto the floor of the island, unable to cope with the pressure. He's now kicking the contents all over the place, into the swamp, destroying everything in his grasp, in his surroundings, *in his life*. He's completely and utterly blind to his own actions and self-destruction.

* * *

As I try to resurrect myself, I come back into the room of the hotel, and everyone is clapping. They must be showing their appreciation to the executives' contribution. I can feel my mobile phone buzzing in my pocket ... it'll be Mike. He'll be leaving me the usual, multiple texts and missed calls as he does every day. Sadly, that's another routine I have to live with.

'Firstly, I want to congratulate you all for being invited here today, because you are all winners and should be proud! You will attend a specific, development program so that we can further support your writing and technical skills. We also didn't feel it was right to just announce the first place either. We want to confirm first, second and third. Are you ready?'

'Okay then ... in no particular order ... Drum-roll.... Come on....' he continues.

We all make a drum-roll noise with our tongues.

'We picked this piece of work because of the technical side. The way in which pictures have been used to make insurance more fun is credible. David Smith come to the front!'

We all cheer as David gets up from his chair and walks to the front of the room.

'This next piece of work was chosen because it involved both animation and documentation. A lot of work has gone into this. Sophie Baker, come to the front of the room!'

We all cheer again as Sophie makes her way to the front.

'This last piece of work was brilliant because it brings insurance to the people. It is simply laid out, cheap to develop, cost-effective and links into the internet. Rather than producing expensive, bulky booklets, this gives an overview of what is available, and the customer can go onto our web-site or request a booklet if they want more in-depth information. Lucy Boardman, come to the front of the room!'

I sheepishly walk forward; awkward, shy Sophie and ultra-confident David smile politely at each other.

'Okay then; this has been difficult due to the high quality of your applications. It was a unanimous decision though. This product was real in terms of what we could produce and offer our customers. We also felt that we could bring this into our operation quickly. Without further ado, the winner is ... Lucy Boardman!'

Too excited to feel embarrassed, I gladly accept my prize. They tell me that they were impressed with my writing technique. Does that mean that I do have a skill with writing? Who knows, but there's one thing I do know; I'll certainly enjoy spending the £2000!

Chapter 4

Jenny's start date is delayed for one week, due to training on another new system. She'll want to be on full power when she gets here, so I can understand why she wants to know everything about our systems and no doubt *us*. She's probably rummaging through our bins now as we're sat in work. I'll give her eight weeks; she'll run out of steam, like a boxer who gives too much in the first few rounds.

'That's all I need,' I think to myself, as I read an email from Jenny. Work is hard enough these days without her making it feel worse, claustrophobic, completely and utterly un-inspiring as the last sediments of any interest remaining just so happened to reveal itself this very second, only to have the door well and truly slammed in its face, never to be opened again. I look across to Susan; she's sat at the workstation to the left of me. She's robotically counting money and placing it into her cash-drawer. Her deep red, cropped hair glistens as the sun sweeps overhead. Heavily made-up, green eyes magnify behind her black-rimmed glasses. Her tweed skirt, thick tights and bulky shoes give her age away. She could dress years younger than she is with her wrinkle-free skin and amazing complexion, smooth, delicate, make her look years younger. Blush exaggerates her cheekbones, and the colour matches her maroon cardigan. Continue to read my emails; I have one from a head-office executive, he's copied Jenny and Rick into it. Apparently, they're that impressed with my 'easy guide to insurance', he wants me to go and see him. I can tell Jenny doesn't like that fact, especially by the tone of her email. Even though she's not here in person, she's here in email:

Hi Lucy

Sorry I cannot authorise a day out of the office, not until I am confident there is no risk to

Customer Service. Let me settle in for a few weeks and I'll see if there is another

opportunity for you in the next few months.

Jenny

'What a control freak. She definitely doesn't want to empower anyone,' I sigh to myself. I smile as I read an email from Rick, congratulating me on my opportunity. I email him back.

Hi Rick

I'm not going to Manchester as Jenny can't authorise the day for me. She said she wants

to settle in first and will look at giving me a chance in a few months.

Thanks anyway

Lucy

Feel annoyed as the phone on my workstation starts ringing and a part of me doesn't want to answer it. I stare, praying the ringing will stop, but no such luck. I begrudgingly pick it up.

'Good morning, Lucy speaking,' I answer, with a false *happy to be here* tone in my voice.

'Lucy, it's Rick. I'm sorry but I can't allow you to miss this opportunity. Jenny isn't the boss yet, not until she arrives. I've arranged cover for you; I'm sending someone from my branch. So you are going to Manchester for the day.'

'I don't want any trouble, Rick.'

'Lucy, it is an order. Stop worrying and just go; I'll let Jenny know,' Rick says, and then ends the call.

Rick always looked out for me; we had a connection, not in a sexual way, and we never even had conversations about that. I think it was a mutual respect for whatever reason; it was instant from the start.

* * *

Sat on the train, travelling to Manchester city centre, I have a sense of freedom, even if it is for just one day....

Sharpness against my shoulders and down my spine, as thick bark ridges press into my back like a bed of nails protruding against the weight of my body as I try to lean back against the trunk of the tree. Soaking wet, through to my skin; muddied water gelled to my hands and arms and glued to my hair. A dream-like atmosphere, captivated within a blanket of pure-white, illuminated, early-morning mist. Completely surrounded by large fern plants and ivy, the greenness of the foliage appears blacker in colour. Blanket mist prevents me from seeing anything further; it is protecting and containing me in the spot where I'm sat.

Look out of the window as the train journeys to the big city. No longer in familiar territory; gasp in awe and amazement as the train storms through a jungle-like place. Clinging onto the metal headrest as the train smashes its way through the tough, tangled, jungle branches. Screaming, screeching metal, searing into my ears. Earth shattering windows; smashing against thick, torn, uprooted branches. Frightening, deafening, grinding and snapping sounds, as the train rips the jungle apart as easily as a lawnmower cutting grass. Desperately hanging on, as leathery leaves are torn from the branches. A huge impact explodes into the carriage and lifts me off the floor.

I wake up in a crumpled mess on the other side of the aisle, on the floor, underneath the table that's fixed between the seats. I recognise the smell of putrid, stinking, dirty swamp water. Mist is rolling into the train via the half-open door ... I gingerly crawl out from under the table, surprised I've not broken a bone in my body. None of this makes sense to me, dreaded confusion consumes the air I struggle to breathe, as I stand up and look out of the cracked window. Leaning against the broken glass, I plunge forward as it smashes out of the window-frame and into the jungle. Peer out of the frame and gaze towards a faint outline of trees, a stunning exposure against the orange, hazy sky. One solid tree stands out in the distance exuding strength and stability amongst the trail of destruction. Its true-blackness and height is a centrepiece beckoning me to journey towards it. But I can't even differentiate between hard jungle floor and dirty swamp water. Deadly silence is broken by the cry of the twisted metal as it settles beneath the carnage. I look around and realise I am the only passenger; there's only me here. With my head sticking out of the open window I look towards the front of the train as a figure stumbles out of the first carriage. Grappling with the seats, I push myself away from the window frame and pull myself towards the half-open door. Hesitantly step down to feel if the ground is solid or swamp. It is solid, dry mud which is as hard as concrete as I feel it under foot. Broken foliage still clinging onto the torn branches, dying and tortured; time will ensure they rot into the heart of the jungle.

Suffocating, poisonous atmosphere; billowing, fuel-filled, black smoke; wafting it with my left hand, and have my right hand covering my nose and mouth. Stumbling away from the thick smoke I step backwards to take in the absolute carnage of the train crash ... the front carriage impacted with the face of the cliff. The last four carriages are lying on their side amongst the smoke and torn earth. I can't believe what I'm seeing, to be back here at the edge of the cliff. Wetness in my stride as I realise I'm stepping backwards into the swamp water. I place my hands on my head in confusion as I hurry away from the disgusting fumes and towards the front of the train. The figure that emerged from the first carriage is powering ahead towards the furthest end of the cliff face. Maybe he wasn't injured after all. Why has the train driven me back to the edge of the swamp? The train driver is scurrying towards what looks like an entrance to a cave. Sickly, uncomfortable feeling in the pit of my stomach; I feel as if the sky is closing in. Darkness has suddenly set in and I feel as if the focus is on me, but I don't know who is watching. Fear is holding my hand and pulling me along; with its arm around my waist ... the shadow Fear casts is pitch-black, and it is forcing me forward.

I look back towards the swamp ... the atmosphere is dead, completely broken and lost amongst the smoke and mist. Distracted by the distant light within the cave, I know I have to enter. I feel my way in by shimmying along the right side of the cave wall. Fear is tormenting me, whispering in my ear, telling me I'm going to see something I may not like. It now wants me to turn around and run, as I always do, but I have to see this for myself. The inner walls of the cave have narrowed and I'm feeling the stone-cold hardness with my hands as I walk. They feel smooth, yet uneven ... there's just enough room to walk through this part of the cave. I reach the light that is beaming out of a doorway. I sink to the floor when I peer through and realise the train driver is actually Mike. He's got a grip of me, squeezing my wrists, pinning me up against the wall in the kitchen. His face is millimetres away from mine as he hurls vile, verbal abuse and I desperately want him to let go. I'm kicking his legs, pleading with him to leave me alone. But he can't see or hear my pleading; he's completely blind to it. He's shaking me and forcing me backwards ...he lets go of my wrists and I lash out at his face trying my best to force him away.

'What would people think if they knew you were hitting me?' he sneers at me.

But I see it now ... I can see it from here. He does this to me every night as soon as I walk in from work. There's no explanation from him as to why he does it, it's just something I've come to expect. It's part of my every-evening routine, in the same context as deciding what to have to eat.

'You can't say that to me anymore! I can see what you're doing to me. You've been very clever ... you're in my face, you're in my space. So, I've *not* been attacking you; I've been *protecting* myself. I see it clearly for the first time!' I shout back, as I sit on the floor looking at my red-raw wrists.

'I see what you're doing to me!' I cry.

Mike can't answer ... maybe he didn't see it either?

'You're talking fucking shit; no one will believe you,' he shouts, as he storms out of the house.

I can't run into my field ... I can't get to it; I have nowhere to hide any more, I *can't* hide. Stand up to walk out of the cave, looking back at myself in a crumpled mess on the kitchen floor. Feeling like a victim, I know I deserve better than this. Wanting to walk over and drag myself up from the kitchen floor, brush myself down and act with pride but I know I can't. Stuck solid, all I can do is stare at me as I sit confused in the wonder of the bizarre and horrific world I've been living in. Seeing enough, I walk out feeling confused as I stagger towards the edge of the swamp. I don't stop to think; I can't think straight. The smoke from the crashed train has cleared but it looks as disabled as a washed-up, stranded whale ... it's absolutely huge in size and looks completely out of place here. Sitting at the edge of the swamp water I look out across at what is left of the first island. The swamp water is very shallow; the stench is disgusting. It looks and smells more like raw sewerage. I know I'm going to have to walk through all of this to get back to the third island. I'm not sure why I've been dragged back here; maybe I'm not learning; maybe I'm not really moving forward or making enough effort to find a solution. My stomach heaves as I take my first step into the shallow, thick sewerage. Burning legs, as the acid liquid soaks through to my skin. Hands held above my head, slowly wade deeper into the turgid mess. Mike's laughter forces me to look back; he's stood at the edge of the swamp. He can't believe I'm being this stupid.

'You stupid idiot! You'll never make it; you'll never make a life without me.'

I'd rather walk through this acid, stinking mess which is now at waist height. Hundreds of flies, buzzing into my face and around my head; everywhere. Freaked-out, but I have to think about every move I make. Block out the pain as I slowly and gingerly move forward. Instant relief as I edge my way past the first island. The swamp has watered down; the consistency isn't as thick or disgusting. Mike is too much of a coward to follow me. He's stomping back towards his cave. He looks like he's carrying a dead animal in his right hand. I watch from the swamp water as he places his two hands around it and rings its neck. Shaking it, he then discards it on the ground, as if it means nothing to him. It doesn't make sense to me, so I turn to face the second island and focus on making my way there.

* * *

I've never been to our Manchester branch; it's in a brand-new building and Manchester has been massively developed so there's some amazing, modern architecture that is quite breath-taking. I gaze up at the buildings as I make my way to meet the executive. It's nice to be in a bit of hustle-and-bustle, though a sharp wind is encasing my body in an outer shell of ice, so I wish I'd put on my big coat. Push rotating doors and walk into the reception area; expansive space with sleek, black, marble-tiled flooring. Coffee counter at one corner, cream-coloured, leather settees and chairs dotted around, as people group in their huddles. Approach the receptionist, when I hear a voice, shouting my name. 'Lucy' echoes within the air around me and I lose myself for a moment, unsure if I'm actually in Manchester or struggling within the swamp waters. Smile with relief as I spin round and see the executive standing there.

'I was just getting a coffee, do you want one?' he asks.

'Sure, thanks.'

We walk over to the coffee counter. I'm glad I made the effort to get smartly dressed today as he's stood next to me in his gleaming, pinstriped suit. He's wearing a full suit including waistcoat, and a chain is fixed into one pocket so I can only presume it's a pocket-watch. He has stiffly gelled, black hair that's swept back from his face. He does look like an Italian member of the Mob. I'm sure he's not! Overpowering aftershave, just glad it smells nice; it smells of expense. Step into the lift, head-to-toe in clear glass. I look down, towards the expansive reception, with its huge, modern chandelier hanging down from the centre. Awkwardness in complete silence before stepping out of the lift and walk down an open-spaced hallway.

'We're in here,' he says, as he opens a door and lets me walk in. His office is super-modern, with a sleek, black marble-effect desk and three executive-black, leather, high-back chairs.

'Take off your jacket and make yourself comfortable,' he says, as he reaches his hand out to take it off me.

I remove it with such intent speed and urgency in passing it to him that his hand practically touches mine. He hangs it up on a free-standing coat-stand and removes his suit jacket; opens a door of what I thought was a floor-to-ceiling cupboard for storage but surprised to see that it's a wardrobe. He places his suit jacket onto a hanger and hangs it up in there. A heartbeat, thumping with alarm as he removes his waistcoat and loosens his tie; removing it with a flourish that is so slick, you'd miss it in a blink of an eye. I look over at the door, hoping it isn't locked. If he starts taking off his shirt, I can make a run for it. To my relief, he stops at the tie, but not before he unbuttons the top two buttons of his shirt and then rolls up the sleeves to his elbows. I wouldn't mind but it's not as if it's even too hot. The room temperature is tepid and no more than that. I just hope he's not wearing those rip-and-strip trousers. You know the ones; one yank of his hand and they're off in a swoop.

'Okay Lucy, I guess you're wondering why I invited you here today,' he says, as he finally sits in his chair to face me and takes a huge gulp of his hot coffee, nearly choking in the process. I'm trying my best to keep a straight face.

'I am,' I answer, as best I can, desperately looking for something other than his spluttering on which I can focus. I'm distracted by the wet patch on his shirt which looks like it has dribbled out of his left nipple. He's not wearing a bra under his shirt. Maybe he wears nipple-clamps in his spare time and one nipple has got infected. He starts to wipe the patch with his handkerchief, unimpressed with my constant gawping.

'Bloody coffee,' he says, as he continues to wipe it.

He gets up out of his chair; I'm half-expecting him to ask me to leave, but he steps into the wardrobe and out of sight. I hope it isn't one of those naughty chambers, a multitude of shackles hanging down. He'll tie himself up, shout me over, begging me to whip him senseless. He suddenly walks out, buttoning-up a crisp, fresh shirt.

'Sorry about that,' he says, as he sits back down.

'Be here now, be here now,' I remind myself, I gulp my coffee, hoping the caffeine will wake me up.

'Okay Lucy. I asked you here today because I am really impressed with your writing skills,' he announces, and then more carefully sips his coffee. 'I was talking to Rick, as he was your previous manager and he agrees that you have a skill.'

Double-check for bra-straps as he stands up and walks towards the large, rectangular window. Perversely examining his every move in stunned silence. He swoops around, which snaps me out of my trance in an instant. His blue eyes are transfixed on mine, quite hypnotic as they standout against his fake-tanned skin and bleached-white teeth.

'There's a vacancy here in Manchester; basically it's for the advertising side of the business. The product is developed and then it's handed to this team to work on the advertising format. I'd like you to spend today with that team to see if you think it is somewhere you would like to work. If you do like it, I would like you to apply for the position available. Obviously, you will have to go through the interview process,' he says.

'Of course,' I answer.

'I'll take you to them now,' he says, as he stands next to me, politely urging me to stand up before he throws me out of the room. I put my bag strap on my shoulder and lift my coat up from the coat stand, as he leads me out of his office and down the corridor.

'I'll leave you with these guys,' he says, as he opens a door and lets me walk in.

He turns to leave and the door closes behind me. I feel like I've been hurled out of a moving car and left for dead; standing alone, looking around the room as people busy around me. A hot, stuffy room; lots of talking and movement, but faces look hazy and featureless. It must be my nerves. The next two hours fly by and I love it; working with a group of ten other people, some of whom are the technical guys; a couple are amazing computer animation artists. There are two young girls who take calls and do the admin work. The other three are working with me on producing the written material that sits behind the product and advertises it; make it stand-out from the crowd. It feels like I'm home; feeling truly alive as my innermost being yearns to escape from the body it's been trapped within; scared to open my mouth too wide in case the feelings spill out and leave me for an eternity.

The four of us decide to go out into the city for lunch. The brisk, fresh air feels amazing, filtering right through my body, oxygenating. We're sat outside a restaurant that has a lunch-time menu, and we opt for a warm, seafood salad. We sit alongside the water's edge as it flows past within the canal. The water looks dark, deep and forbidding. So glad there's a metal barrier that separates us from the water's edge. Familiar scent of putrid swamp enters my airways; look up at the three faces around the small, wooden table; they don't make sense to me; melting, drooped, expressionless faces. Look up, into the sky to make sure the sun isn't torching them, but there's no sign of any sun. If anything, the air seems to have darkened and it's freaking me out. Immediately get off my chair and walk towards the metal barrier; can't bear to look at them anymore. Glistening water is a welcome distraction, glistening like cut-glass diamonds, as light sweeps over it. I look up into the sky, confronted by the expansive full moon, glaring at me in its anger. That's odd! Ducks, pecking against the stone lining of the canal-side. I grab a breadstick off our table and lean against the chest-high barrier; force my arm downwards to place the bread-stick in the duck's beak. Step onto the lower rail to stretch further downward and lean precariously over ... a sudden unsteady silence. I flip over the edge.

Plunge deep under the murky water, in a battle for life. Frantically trying to reach out for something, anything, that will help me get back up to the surface. I manage to grab hold of what feels like a rope. The rope isn't moving though. I pull myself up; a race against time, as the putrid water enters my lungs. Thick, greasy, slimy rope; this is my last stretch. My hand suddenly feels ice-cold; it must be out of the water. With one final stretch upwards I force my head out, the slimy, thick fluid vomits out of my mouth. Thickly layered gunk covers my face and body.

Intense heat tightens and dries the gunk and I feel as if I'm turning to stone; crackling on my body as it tightens further. Shifting and moving every muscle in my face as the hardened gunk cracks and starts to fall off. Astonishing realisation as I look around; can't quite believe what I'm seeing. I'm in the jungle, fallen from the third island, hanging onto the rope-like branches within the swamp water. Confused, not knowing if I fell asleep and fell in, or if my journey became too exhausting. Did I even travel to Manchester? Sickly exhaustion as I contemplate my journey to the fourth island; looking back, the third island is nearer and someone is sat on it. Pitiful sorrow as tears start to roll; being forced to stay in a life I don't want. Wipe the tears away and look at my hands; they're red in colour. Wipe my face again; the red is a deeper colour. Look up and realise I'm sat on my bedroom floor; pushed out of bed. I must have hit the wall and my nose is bleeding. Mike mutters something under his vile breath and collapses back down on the bed in his drunken state.

Quietly walk into the bathroom and sit on the edge of the bath. Look at myself in the mirror; there's not that much blood - probably seemed worse because I was half asleep. Maybe I just fell out of bed or was taking up too much room and he was heavy-handed when he was moving me out of the way. Wash my face and sit in a trance as I stare into the mirror, not really looking at anything, not even myself.

The figure seems to be someone I recognise but I'm not sure as I clamber up onto the third island and sit, staring. Gaze towards it from behind as its back leans against the trunk. Shiver as the grey tinge on the right arm and hand illuminates within the brightness of the naked, pale flesh. I've never seen a dead body before. Too scared to approach it, I stay and stare, analysing for any movement. The jungle wind is piercing my back, forcing me to move, battering me from behind and trying to lift me up off the floor of the island. I slowly crawl towards the figure, approaching from the side, absolutely petrified. Close enough to reach out and touch the hand.

'Hello,' I whisper.

No movement as I slowly reach out to touch the hand with my forefinger; I can feel the softness of the skin when I prod it. It has to be alive then. I take a deep breath and slowly crawl to the side of it, almost too scared to look across, but I have to. The fragile, empty, greying figure sort of looks like me; limp hair, stuck solidly to each side of the face. Lifeless, colourless eyes. I kneel in front and pull it towards me; hold it in my arms. A freezing, empty body that clearly needs care and love; hold it slightly away, looking for signs of life. Place my hand on each shoulder and gently shake, but the head just rocks backwards and practically disappears from my sight. I gently lay the body back against the trunk of the tree and hold both hands within mine. Expressionless eyes stare out, right through me; it has completely and utterly shut itself off from the world. I turn myself around and sit on its knees and sink within its frame. Our bodies merge and I look down at the right arm and hand, as the bluish tinge slowly disappears and the arm returns to its frigid, white colour.

I look up at the bedroom door, knowing I have to walk through it, take one last look at my arms and hands. Snoring Mike has taken over the whole bed; a dead-weight and the familiar stench of putrid alcohol consumes the room. Quietly lie down on the edge of the bed, it dawns on me that if the Manchester thing was all a dream, it means that Jenny will be working at our branch from tomorrow. Something I'm not looking forward to, and it stops me from getting back to sleep. I check my mobile for the time, its 4:30 a.m. Mike normally falls asleep downstairs. The cold must have woken him from his drunken coma and brought him to bed.

* * *

As I walk towards the bank, I'm surprised there's no red carpet, no red ribbon and large, gold scissors to cut it with. No warm-up act standing at a mic, waiting to announce ... no, everything looks normal; but I know there'll be no more normal. Jenny Watkins is arriving today. I take a deep breath and walk through the door. There are no disappointed paparazzi, flashing their cameras, expecting it to be the Infamous Mrs Watkins....

Carol is sitting to attention at the reception desk, wearing a bright-blue blazer, crisp-white blouse and a blooming-red ribbon, tied in a bow at the collar.

'You'll be next,' she says, as I walk towards her, unable to take my eyes off the bow; it's huge. She looks like an air stewardess on steroids.

'I didn't realise it was fancy-dress today. Do I need to go home and get changed,' I tease.

'Piss off!'

'Oooh Carol, that's not like you. Who dressed you today?'

'Her Ladyship is trialling a new uniform. Apparently, she loved the idea that much that she's paid for it herself. Don't worry, she'll have yours on you before you know it,' she continues.

'You're kidding! I mean, we do sort of wear a uniform now. If you can call a white blouse and black skirt or trousers a uniform,' I answer.

'She's that determined we're wearing it, she's brought her sewing-kit and machine in, just in case she needs to take it in. God knows what'll happen if it needs taking out. I wonder how she knew what sizes we were,' Carol muses.

'Don't look at me; this has got nothing to do with me. I've not seen Jenny for a long time,' I sigh.

'Well, I sort of like it, I never get dressed up; I wear the same worn-out trousers and off-white shirts,' Carol says.

'What have you got on your bottoms?' I ask.

'Blue trousers, they're a bit bright, but they don't look too bad indoors. As soon as the sunlight hits them, the colour screams out,' Carol says, as she steps out from behind her desk.

I see what she means.

'What's that on the desk?'

'It's a hairband, it's optional. Jenny brought them in, for a bit of fun. Do you like the earrings too?' Carol asks, as she fingers her hair behind her ears to present her large, red, oval studs.

'Oh well, I'd best make my way up.'

'Good luck.' Carol shouts, as I open the door that leads to the stairs. Delicately step up each stair; I notice the door to Jenny's office is held open by a doorstop. Take a deep breath and sneak past.

'Morning Lucy. Come to my office after you've put your things into your locker,' Jenny demands.

'Morning Jenny,' I answer, and walk into the locker room.

A dazzle of blue hits me as Mary brushes past on her way out. No eye contact; not even a hello. How rude; no doubt she'll dislike the uniform and orders; rules never did apply to her. She was good at her job, always top at sales, so Rick always let her get on with it. I lock my locker, do a couple of stretching exercises. Let me be a size ten or even a twelve, I won't hear the end of it otherwise.

I walk into Jenny's office, stunned at the change.

'How did you manage to change the decor?'

Jenny twirls on her new plum-coloured, leather chair and smiles.

'Do you like it?'

'It's gorgeous; can you come and do mine?' I ask.

'But you don't have an office,' she smirks.

'I meant ... oh, never mind,' I lamely reply.

I take a minute to look around the room; one wall is covered in expensive wallpaper, a plum colour emblazoned with shiny, silver flowers. The other walls are painted in a deep, plush plum; a silver carpet and wooden furniture, lacquered in silver paint.

'How come they let you do this?' I ask, as the bank is normally very strict on anything like this.

'No way was I sitting in it as it was,' she says.

'I had decorators in at the weekend. I had to pay for security to stay in the bank. You'll probably think I've lost the plot, but I've paid for it all. That's how I got it signed off,' she giggles, as she files her nails.

It's then I get my first proper glimpse of her. 'Whatever happened to Baby Jane?' springs to mind. Struggling to keep a straight face, she's got the same garish-blue uniform as the rest of us poor souls, though I've not got mine yet. She's wearing deep-red lipstick on her lips and a thick layer of black eyeliner and sparkling-blue eyeshadow. Bright-red nail varnish on her false nails and an enormous, red flower attached to a hairband on her head. The flower is sat on the side of her head and her flowing, wavy hair is bouncing on her shoulders.

'Your lipstick is smudged everywhere, is it meant to be like that?' I ask, puzzled at the sight.

'Oh God! Let's have a look,' she says, as she grabs a mirror off her desk.

'They could have told me; I look a right freak,' she says.

'That's a relief. I thought you were getting ready to audition for a part in 'Whatever happened to Baby Jane?'

'Lucy, I hope you're not taking the mickey out of me; it wouldn't make a first day, good impression now, would it?' she says, as she tidies up her lipstick with spit on a tissue.

'Of course I'm not Jenny. Come on then, let's have it,' I ask.

'Have what?' Jenny asks.

'My new uniform.'

'I didn't buy you one, you're moving to Manchester for your dream job,' she says, as she stands up and walks towards the door.

I feel a bit uneasy as she locks the door.

'I never got a dream job, that was just what it was - a silly dream,' I say, as I watch her. She is still facing the door which is completely freaking me out.

'What's your problem Jenny?'

'My problem? I'll tell you what my problem is. It's you; everyone always liked you whilst I sat in the background. You were the one being preened and admired at every development program. Even at this last silly project, they were all falling over themselves to say how much they loved your silly little bit of writing. I'm the real talent; I'm the one they got in the end,' she says, as her head turns to look at me, but her body is still facing the door.

'Oh my God, what's going on? What are you?' I ask and move backwards whilst looking for a way out.

'I bet your mother never told you that we have the same daddy, did she?' she continues.

'Help! Help! Can someone hear me?' I scream.

'No one will hear your screams; there's no way out of here. This room is 100% sound-proof,' she seethes.

'Do you want to know who your daddy is?' she says, as her whole body turns to face me.

'It is you; it is you from ''Whatever Happened to Baby Jane,''' I scream.

'I bet your mother never told you that your daddy is dead.'

The smudged lipstick and smudged, over-the-top eyeliner is dripping down her face.

'I've written a letter to Daddy,' she sings, as her head rocks from side to side.

'Enough,' I shout. This isn't real, it can't be real!

I push her away from the door and fight to unlock it, rattling the door handle as freaky-Jenny torments from over my shoulder. I fall out of the door and sit up and find myself sat upright in bed.

'What a nightmare!' I say to myself.

I feel under my pillow for my mobile phone, to check out the time. Shit, it's 9:30. I must have fallen asleep after being rudely awoken. I look across to lifeless Mike; he's in a drunken coma. Jump out of bed; I should have been in work at nine!

It's 10:15 as I step into the taxi.

'Carol, it's Lucy; you won't believe it; I've bleeding well overslept on 'Her Majesty's' first day,' I shout.

'Calm down Lucy, Her Majesty isn't in till eleven o'clock; she said she had a few loose ends to tie up at her previous branch. Hurry, you're missing out; we've got cakes and coffee, celebrating an end of an era. I've saved you a vanilla slice; your favourite, but hurry, it's calling for me to eat it,' Carol laughs.

'Thanks Carol, you're a lifesaver, I owe you big time,' I say, with relief.

'You certainly do, because I've also signed you in,' she whispers.

'Thanks Carol, you're a star; see you in five,' I say, and end the call.

I sit back in the seat, relieved, the panic is over.

I pick up fresh coffees from the High Street coffee shop, and as I approach the door to the bank, I block out thoughts of red carpet. Breathe a huge sigh of relief as I walk towards Carol; she's sat hunched over the reception desk, wearing her usual drab uniform. There isn't a scrap of make-up on her pale face; no bright-red lipstick on her stick-thin lips.

'What are you laughing at?' Carol asks.

'Nothing, you just made me laugh with your coffee and cakes.'

'All's forgiven Lucy, especially as you've brought us some fresh coffee. We need all the caffeine we can get; the only legal-high allowed in this place,' she says, as she reaches for the tray of coffees.

'You'd better go and get your things in your locker and log in, you're probably best telling Jenny that you've been sorting out leaflets or something, she'll probably check sign-in and log-in times,' Carol advises.

'Good thinking; will do,' I say, as I open the door to the stairway and walk upstairs to the locker room.

Pounding heart, beating faster as I realise the door to Jenny's office is held open by a door stop. I stall on the stairs as I contemplate walking past; that nightmare has totally freaked me out. I jump out-of-my-skin as Alan walks out of Jenny's office; he's the mortgage advisor at our branch.

'Alan, you made me jump,' I say, as I continue to walk up the stairs.

Smirking Alan continues to walk down the stairs. He must be six-foot tall with immaculate, blonde hair, cut short at the sides, but layered on top. Pale-blue eyes and wide smile; not very sociable, he prefers to remain in his office on the ground floor.

Sigh as I lock my locker and walk down the stairs and back into reception. Pick up my coffee from Carol's desk, knowing I'll need as much caffeine as possible today.

It's lunchtime before I know it; I can hear the disappointment as I log off to go on my lunch.

'I'll pick up another coffee if you like. I have to go; I'll let Melanie down if I don't.'

'We'll all have hot chocolate, topped with cream,' Carol shouts, with a hint of approval.

'Okay,' I reply, as I step out of the door, a step closer to freedom. Suddenly confronted by Jenny; she's over-loaded with files.

'Thanks Lucy, grab these will you,' she says, and instantly piles the files in my arms.

'Sorry Jenny, but I'm meeting Melanie for lunch,' I say, heaving a sigh of disappointment at the instant expectation from her.

Jenny forces me back into the bank as she follows me, wheeling her trolley-case behind. I place the files on the reception desk to Carol's amazement.

'Can you take them up to my office for me?' Jenny asks.

'Sorry, I'm on my way out, and no doubt it'd be against Health and Safety to expect me to carry files up; I can hardly see over the top of them,' I reply.

'Anyway, Alan's in; ask him. See you later,' I say, as I walk towards the door.

I can feel the heat behind me as I walk away. The cold, fresh air is a welcome relief as I walk up the High Street.

Melanie's familiar frame walks towards me but there's something different about her.

'I like your hair,' I say, as we meet.

'Thanks. I thought it was time for a complete, change,' Melanie says, as she catches a glimpse of her new, cropped haircut in the reflection of a shop window.

We continue our walk together when Andy walks out of his sandwich shop.

'Hi Melanie. Hi Lucy,' he shouts over to us.

'Hi Andy, how is everything?' Melanie shouts over.

'Fine; how are you doing?'

'We're both fine,' Melanie shouts, as we walk past, linking arms.

Before I can look at Melanie to ask, she beats me to it.

'Andy and I had a chat. I went to see him after work on Saturday,' Melanie says.

'I realised after Project Sandwich that I wasn't really angry at him and Rick; it was me that I was angry with,' Melanie sighs.

'Are you okay?' I ask, as we sit down on a bench.

'I felt really depressed for days and it was eating away at me. Then I realised it had opened up unhealed wounds,' Melanie says, with an emotional-toned voice. 'It made me realise that I've not been treating Paul in the right way, and it's all because of my insecurities. I was so petrified of him being unfaithful; I wasn't allowing him to live his life, and I did something awful when he went on a stag-do last weekend,' Melanie whispers.

'What did you do?'

'I destroyed most of his clothes and when he got back, I told him I wanted him to leave. The look on his face will stay with me forever. He could have walked out and left me then, but he proved to be the person he was when we met. He sat me down and told me how he'd been feeling for a while, but because he loved me so much, he just put up with it all.'

'You should have called me Melanie; I feel awful. I had no idea it was torturing you so much,' I say, as I hold her hand.

'Don't you start worrying; it's something I had to figure out for myself. So Paul and I are going to see a relationship counsellor. I want to start living, with Paul,' Melanie continues.

'Well done you; that's very mature and I'm sure you and Paul will live a wonderful life together,' I assure.

'Thanks Lucy, I'm sure we will. Anyway, let's change the subject ... so, how's today been?'

'Jenny's only just arrived, we did literally bump into each other as I was on my way out to meet you. And I refused to help her carry files up the stairs because I was on my lunch. No doubt that'll go against me some time soon.'

'You'll soon find out,' Melanie says, as she takes her sandwiches out of her bag.

'I'm impressed,' I say.

'Why's that?'

'You've actually made yourself a sandwich.'

'I know. Paul and I are going to take it in turns each day. We want to get our health and finances sorted too,' Melanie says, and then takes a bite of her sandwich.

Flourishing trees, growing from within the swamp water; knotted, slime-covered, low-hanging branches. Shuffle down to the edge of the island; fascinated by the entwined, knotted structure protruding. Clear, still waters surrounding the natural climbing-frame of tangled branches stretching upwards; looks like a sinking bridge that links this island to the next.

Sudden movement and rhythmic current urges me to look downwards, beyond my reflection. Hold onto the structure, as I study the view from below, a definite movement, clambering. To my horror, I can see Mike, way down underneath the water, climbing towards me. An urgent fright, knowing I need to move forward now, journey to the fourth island and break the link somehow between this island and the next. Step onto the side of the swaying structure as it struggles to hold the weight of my hold and Mike's determined climb. An uneven balance as I meticulously step within the tough, tangled branches. Urging myself forward, I look back into the distance; a crane lifts the crashed train up off the ground. It is being pulled upwards towards my field. Catch a glimpse of Mike as he pulls himself up onto the top of the structure next to the third island. A mix of panic and determination as I near the fourth island, and jump off the structure, forcing it to move backwards. Unstable movements, and Mike is struggling to keep his balance. Pleading for help, panicking; I have to let him fall this time. Look up towards the large tree and its snaking roots, running along the surface of the island towards the water. Brown-soiled floor is littered with broken branches and decaying leaves. Hold onto the skinny trees that grow out of the steep ground and pull myself upwards, to reach the large trunk. The crusty surface of the trunk is unwelcoming and won't offer me a home or a place to settle. I feel the scaly surface and sit down; delicately lean back against the harsh trunk. Restless and unsettled, I stand up and clamber over the snake-like roots. Weaving through and holding onto the skinny jungle trees; venturing out towards the edge of the island, I need to look out towards the fifth for more comfort.

Looking back, to see what changes I have made to improve my personal life. I'd certainly opened my eyes, to see my life for what it really was. Took control of my finances again; no longer funding Mike's need, no matter what he was putting me through. Knowing I still have a long way to go and decisions to make.

A nudge from Melanie brings me back into the present and back onto the bench, still sat next to her.

'Anyway, it's that time again' Melanie says, as she hugs me goodbye.

'Same time, same place tomorrow,' I say.

'See you tomorrow,' she says, as she gets up off the bench and walks back to work.

'Here she is, and empty-handed too,' Carol says, as I walk into the reception area.

'The coffees; I totally forgot.'

'Well, I'm nipping out now, so hand your money over!' Carol demands, as she holds her hand out.

I take my purse out of my bag and give Carol £10.

'Thanks; and thanks to you, "Her Majesty" is in a right mood! She's locked herself in her office, which is one consolation,' Carol huffs.

'Are you suggesting I put her in that mood?'

'Well, not just you; it was you, Alan and then me. After you refused to help her take the files upstairs, Alan refused because he had a customer waiting. And I told her not to look at me,' Carol announces.

'That's all we need; how did she manage it then,' I ask, as I check my watch; I'm ten minutes late now.

'She shoved past Alan; he was bemused. She stomped her trolley up the stairs and then did two trips up and down the stairs to carry the files.'

'Oh dear,' I say, as I tap in the code to open the door to the stairs.

'I'll be back in about twenty minutes with your coffees, and seeing as Lucy's given £10, I'll try and get us some nice biscuits, or chocolate,' Carol announces.

'I'll never be late again; it costs me too much,' I say, as I close the door behind me.

I creep up the stairs, not wanting to raise the beast. The door is firmly shut; it's a solid door so she won't be able to see me walk past. I put my things in the locker and quickly walk back down the stairs. No movement or sound from the beast, which makes us all a little nervous, not knowing what her next move is.

Leaving for the day, we contemplate checking she is still alive. But they say 'let sleeping dogs lie', so we do.

'Remember girls, we all stick together; we'll get each other through this. And remember, sleep tight, don't have nightmares. See you tomorrow,' Carol says, as she exits the door.

Chapter 5

Step out of bed, put on my dressing-gown and sigh; a sigh that sounds more like a groan. As if before the groan I had momentarily forgotten; forgot my life is in a dreadful state. Then the feeling hits me; the dread, like being hit in the stomach with a cricket bat; as if I've done wrong, something awful; as if it's all my fault. The guilt, feel so guilty; but I never intended my life to turn out like this. I give too much. I know that now, and I know a taker holds no boundaries, they take and take; they are never full, never satisfied, never quite happy; as if every situation is never quite good enough, even small things like something I've cooked, or an idea I have to go somewhere, or to try something new. There's always a negative or a reason why my suggestion is wrong; as if they are a trickster, playing a game and the game is to keep me down; that is their goal. I exhale a deeply, drawn breath as I walk onto the landing. Peering downstairs, illuminated lights; electricity bills have increased; everything's left switched on overnight, every night. Creep downstairs hoping he is still flat out. I don't want to talk or even look at him before I go to work. Heavy breathing, sweltering bulk and blood-red face tells me he's not been unconscious for too long. Three empty wine-bottles stand on the floor. The TV is still switched on, but on silent mode; remote controls on the floor, one is lying in spilled red wine, the other is in the middle of the floor with batteries smashed out of the back. I really can't stand living like this anymore. Scratching at the back door as I walk into the kitchen, the poor dog has been left out, and he comes clambering into the house as I open the door, looking cold and desperate for a hug. No desire to hang around or communicate with Mike, I walk back upstairs to shower and get ready for work.

'*Yooohoooo*,' Carol shouts, as I'm about to walk into the coffee shop.

'Hi Carol.'

'Just the person. I heard some major gossip last night and I wanted you to be the first to know,' Carol gushes, as she gently pushes me into the coffee shop. 'I'll get the coffee today; you go and get a table,' she continues.

I sit at a table near the window and stare out onto the High Street. It's only 8:15, and so nice to sit in peace and quiet, with my elbows on the table, cupping my face in the palms of my hands as I stare out at nothing.

The peace and quiet comes to an abrupt end when Carol slams the tray onto our table.

'Was there any need for that?' I ask.

'For what,' Carol says, unaware of her loudness.

I watch as she lifts our mugs of coffee off the tray and throws the packets of sugar and milk into the middle of the table. Finally, she lifts a little plate of toasted teacakes and puts them next to her coffee. She throws the tray onto the table next to ours, rips open four packets of sugar and milk and stirs her coffee for what seems like ten minutes. The clank of the spoon against her mug is irritating me. Carol is just too annoying first thing in the morning. I won't be doing this again, that's for sure. No table-manners either; she eats open-mouthed; half a toasted teacake eaten in one bite. Forgetting where she is, the butter dripping down her chin, she licks it off with her tongue.

'Carol!' I say, in disgust.

'Sorry Lucy, I'm bloody starving. I was on the phone for most of the night last night and didn't eat a thing.'

'What's this gossip anyway?' I ask.

'That's why I was on the phone all night; it's about Rick.'

I purposely pick up my mug of black coffee and take a sip. At least if I hide my mouth, she won't see a reaction. It can't be about 'Project Sandwich'; she shouldn't know anything about that. I'm sure Melanie would never have mentioned it to anyone.

'What about Rick?' I ask, and then continue to sip and listen.

'Rick and Victoria have split up,' Carol announces, as she picks up another piece of toasted tea cake.

I don't know what's worse, praying she doesn't know anything about the Project, or watching her eat. No wonder she lives on her own.

'You eat and drink too fast,' I squirm.

She wipes her hands on a napkin; the butter is everywhere.

'Sorry Lucy; I'm starving.'

'Right, where were we? Okay, I was speaking to Adele who works in the music shop on the High Street. She said she saw Victoria and she looked awful. She thought it was because she's pregnant; you know how hard it can be. She decided to go and see her to see if she could help in any way. They were best mates at school, but lost touch when she married Rick. She said Victoria thought she was better than everyone, especially when she moved into that big house. Anyway, when she went round, Victoria broke down and told her that Rick had left a week earlier,' Carol continues.

'Did Adele say anything else? Is anyone else involved?'

'Well, that's where I'm hoping you can help.'

'Me, how can I help?'

'Well, we all know how close you and Rick are, surely you must know something?' Carol asks, and examines my eyes, searching for an answer.

'Rick and I were close on a professional level only. Why would Rick tell me anything about his personal life?'

'I'm only asking Lucy. Anyway, I might as well tell you; Adele said that Victoria asked her if she'd seen him with any other women.'

'And?'

'Well, Adele said she'd seen Rick a couple of times with Andy in the music shop, but never any women. Andy and Rick are mates from school, so Victoria reckons he may know who this other woman is. Adele was asking me questions about you,' Carol sheepishly announces.

'Why me?'

'Victoria's adamant that another woman must be involved, apparently, she and Rick haven't had sex for about six months. She put it down to being pregnant, but she reckons they never had much of a sex life before that either,' Carol announces.

'And I want to know about this because ...?' I ask.

'Well, Victoria reckons Rick spoke about you a lot, so I'm just pre-warning you,' Carol continues.

'Oh, for God's sake, that's ridiculous.'

'I know that, but just thought you should know,' Carol says, as she piles our mugs on top of each other and places them on top of the little plate.

'Well, I'd say it was nice having coffee with you, but I never expected this,' I say, feeling really annoyed.

'Sorry Lucy, I thought you would want to know; I know I would,' Carol replies.

'No, it's not you. Thanks for telling me, I really appreciate it. I wish more people were more honest,' I say, as I get up from my chair.

'Is that the time already?' I say, as I look at my watch and see it is 8:50 am.

'Well, I honestly don't know anything about Rick and another woman. I'll ask Melanie if she knows anything; I'll be catching up with her for lunch,' I say, as we walk to the door.

'Oh yeah, let me know.'

I can't believe it. Why should I take the blame for the break-up of Rick and Victoria's marriage? Rumours like this can be damaging to reputations. I certainly don't want that. Just wait till I tell Melanie; she'll know what to do. Just hope I don't bump into Victoria; cheeky bitch, how dare she even think that. I see Adele never twigged about Rick and Andy, but she never was the brightest star in school. That wouldn't have even crossed her mind. Rick doesn't look like a stereotypical gay man; but what would I know? Just wait till I hear from him. Imagine if this got back to Mike. He's insecure enough as it is; would he believe the 'Andy and Rick' tale? He'd probably think it was bullshit. Maybe I should go and see Victoria myself; tell her I've been told about her and Rick and that I know she's been asking questions about me. I think I will, but I'll see what Melanie thinks first; not that I'd get a level-headed answer from her; she can't stand Victoria at the moment. That's it, rant over!

It's Tuesday; the bank doesn't open its doors to customers until 9:30. I wonder what Jenny's got in store for us?

'What's going on? Mary and Susan are stood outside the bank,' Carol says, as we near. The early-morning traffic is at a stand-still. The dirty, grey pavements are littered with empty take-away cartons and a splash of vomit. The High Street pub has a Monday night, happy drinking hour to encourage more trade.

'Oh yeah; it looks like Jenny's not in yet then,' I reply.

Carol picks up speed, hoping for a drama. 'What's going on girls?'

'Jenny's in. We saw her flitting through the door, to go upstairs. But that was ten minutes ago,' Mary says, as she peers through the glass door.

'Have you rung the bell?' Carol asks.

'We didn't like to. She did see us, so she knows we're standing here,' Mary says.

Mary never likes to create a fuss; she looks as timid as a mouse. Her short-layered, golden-blonde hair is tucked behind her ears; long fringe sweeps to the right of her face. Sculptured eyebrows crown her oval, brown eyes and she has a dusting of makeup on her pale skin and natural-coloured lips. She doesn't talk unless she's being spoken to; she needs to spend more time with Carol.

'She's playing games with us girls; she's already bought the ticket for her power-trip and we're allowing her to get on board,' Carol announces triumphantly.

'What else can we do?' Mary asks, looking slightly amused and relieved. As if she's glad someone's there to take control of the situation.

'Ring the bell girls, ring the bell,' Carol instructs. As she forcefully presses her finger onto the bell, the tip of her finger goes white.

Susan places her hand over her mouth as she looks on in disbelief.

'This is how it's done girls!' Carol announces, as she continues to leave her finger firmly on the bell and takes hold of her mobile phone. 'Hi Jenny, what's going on? We're waiting to come in. My finger's getting sore ... okay Jenny, see you in a minute,' she says, and puts her phone back in her bag. Takes her finger off the bell button, but it looks like it's still pressed inwards. We're unable to hear whether it's still ringing, as the sounder is upstairs and not within the reception downstairs.

'What did she say?' I ask.

'She said she was just photocopying and was on her way down.'

Jenny walks towards the door and unlocks it; holding it open as we all walk in.

'Good morning, everyone,' she says, without eye contact. 'We'll go into my office, just head up there while I lock the door.'

Smirking faces, ear-numbing clanging of the bell, as we walk up the stairs.

'*Ooops,*' Carol says, as she puts her fingers in her ears. 'Sorry Jenny!'

'It's okay Carol, I'll disconnect it from up here.'

'Okay then. Firstly, I'm sorry I wasn't in yesterday morning; I never got chance to speak to you all on my first day. What must you think of me? I just want to talk you through the new holiday system; I know it's not exciting, but Rick should have done this months ago. Talk about being disorganised,' she hisses, as she hands out copies of instructions, and talks to us as if we are toddlers. The presentation goes by in a haze as Jenny refuses to even look at me.

'I'll go and buy you all a drink,' Jenny says, as she leads us back downstairs.

As we walk into the reception area, windswept Alan fumes as he stands outside, absolutely unimpressed. A face like thunder as Jenny unlocks the door.

'Sorry Alan, blame Carol; she broke the bell. I really hope you've not been stood there for long.'

'I've been stood here for twenty minutes. I've got clients coming in soon and I wanted to prepare beforehand. I wouldn't mind, but I have a key; someone put the double lock on,' Alan moans.

'Oh, sorry Alan; that must have been me, but I am still getting used to the door,' Jenny laughs smugly.

Awkward silence, as Alan storms through reception and into his office.

'Carol, if my clients arrive will you apologise and let them know I'll be twenty minutes. Oh, and can you make them a drink,' he shouts.

'No problem, Alan,' Carol shouts back, and sits behind the reception desk.

'Does Alan always expect you to get a drink for his clients?' Jenny asks Carol.

'Not really, he's normally so organised.'

'I'll be back in a minute with those drinks,' Jenny says, as she disappears out of the door.

Absolute silence as we log into our workstations; so disappointingly predictable. Jenny's arrival has definitely changed this place forever.

'Here you go,' Jenny shouts, as she returns carrying a tray of coffees. 'I got white coffees all round. Sorry Lucy, I've just realised you only drink black coffee, don't you?'

'It's okay; I had a coffee just before I got here.'

'You must be here to see Alan? He's 10 minutes late; you can have this fresh coffee; sit down and relax,' Jenny gushes, to customers, passing them the coffee and smirking as she walks past me.

* * *

'She's driving me round the bend,' I wail to Melanie, as we meet for our usual lunchtime catch-up.

'You're just being paranoid; give it a few more days,' Melanie reassures.

'I've got enough on my plate at the moment. Rick's offered me a job at his branch and even said I could work one day at home each week, but I've been told that Victoria thinks Rick and I are having an affair!' I rant.

'Hang on, back up. Okay, firstly, you never told me that Rick offered you a job and what's this about Rick and that bloody Victoria?'

'I only found out this morning; apparently Rick left Victoria and they never had much of a sex life, so Victoria is adamant Rick left her for another woman. She also said that he spoke about me a lot and is putting two and two together and coming up with one hundred,' I sigh.

'You've got to put Victoria straight; why should you take the rap for this?' Melanie demands.

'And what about this job? You never mentioned anything. You do know you'll never get a better lunchtime buddy?'

'I know, I'm sorry. I've not put much thought into it. It was a throw-away comment that Rick made. He reckons I'll want to move once Jenny gets her claws into us at our branch, and I think he might be right. I feel completely suffocated and she's not really started yet, I feel trapped,' I sigh.

Prodding and splashing the swamp waters with a thin, gangly, jungle branch. Slumped at the edge of the fourth island; looking out towards the vast greenery on the fifth and the surrounding waters.

A sudden change in the atmosphere; it's being pulled away from the centre of where I'm sitting. Stunned, I feel panic inside; I can just about see the island in the distance, but it looks too far out at sea. Exhausted, I clamber into the swamp water with Fear pushing from behind. Frantically trying to stay afloat as I use my arms and legs to wade forwards; but the island is moving farther away. Ready to drown, not caring enough about myself; ignoring the things that are going on around me. Floating on the surface of the waters, I realise I'm not being honest with myself. Looking up into the sky at the unsteady blend of black and grey clouds; looks as harsh as the aftermath of a world war. Burnt-orange sky and tender whiteness of fresh clouds trying to break through; filtered light growing in the distance. A touch of blue sky emerging behind the whiteness of the clouds but seems so far away.

My lifeless body lies in bed; I feel completely lost. I need to find myself, but how can I find something that is not lost, but already visible to the eye and touch? My body feels as fragile as an empty eggshell. I have fallen. I feel what I need to feel. My body has finally broken.

My life in the jungle has merged with my life outside of it. It was on countdown from the moment I landed on the jungle floor. My soul is defeated, and I can't go on and live my life the way I have been. My name is Lucy Boardman, and I am NOT a robot. I repeat, I am NOT a robot.

Back from where I've been floating, I hear Mike shout my name, but I'm completely unresponsive; his voice sounds far away. My body is moulded onto the floor of the fifth island; I can feel the earth between my lifeless fingers. It feels cold and grainy. I'm washed ashore, shipwrecked; the jungle branches have started to encase my body; they are twining themselves around my legs, slowly and gently pulling me back into the swamp waters. They want to drag me back and keep me there forever. It is then I start to awake from my coma. I don't want to be lost forever in this place or fight my way out of the swamp. I've got to get up and find the energy to get to the sixth island, to move forward and get out of here. It's not going to be easy, but I've got to deal with the things that keep me here, so that once I'm out, I'm out forever.

Sit up, amazed at the vast amount of greenery; this island is different ... can't get near the trunk of the jungle tree. Light-green shrubbery with shiny leaves and red berries surround the area; darker-green foliage with red tinges on each leaf cover the entire trunk. Smaller bushes with pale-yellow leaves ... shrubs with olive-green leaves shaped like tiny hands. Total blackness engulfs the air between the different elements of the foliage. A misty opening to the right of the trunk beckons me forward; careful with each step so I don't get tangled underfoot.

Weak, breathless; step out of bed and into the bathroom. The warm water feels welcoming as I close my eyes and lie down in the bath. No desire to move, so I top it up with hot water, twisting the tap with my foot. So relaxing as I lie in the scorching-hot water. I sigh, knowing I can't stay here forever.

Feeling the leaves as I walk through with trepidation; rope-like branches hang down from the bulking branches that tower above. I move into a clearing surrounded by low-lying, green fern and ivy. Warmth; feel warmth within this atmosphere.

Dry myself down with wrinkled fingers; grab hold of the jungle tree and look towards the sixth island. Surprised at how close it actually is; need to have more faith in myself. A stream of brown-coloured swamp water flows past and separates the two islands. Rocks protrude, in a line, like stepping-stones. The deep-orange sun is blazing down on my face and the warm wind is blowing at my hair; the warmth feels comforting, a feeling I never thought I would feel again. Gazing, I could stand here forever; shield my eyes as the sun blazes from beyond the jungle trees. It is filtering between the branches and touches the swamp, as the rays filter out across the whole of the jungle floor. It looks and feels amazing, but I know it won't last forever; the sun comes and goes as it pleases. Tightening skin and dry mouth, so I close the bathroom blind. No idea how long I've been stood here.

Walk downstairs; quite a novelty that I have the house to myself. Quality time on my own in the house I work so hard for; I realise my life has gone downhill since that time stopped; need to be alone sometimes. I turn on my mobile and the message box quickly fills with messages from close friends. There are a few messages from Rick; opening the first, it reads:

Hi Lucy, sorry Rick hasn't returned your call; he left his phone at home when he left me and hasn't been back since.

Victoria.

'That's all I need,' I say, as I read the other messages sent from Rick's phone.

Hi Lucy, it's Victoria. I was hoping for a response to my last message. Can you please ring me when you get this?

Lucy, I really need to talk to you, you've got nothing to worry about, please return my call.

The fourth message reads:

How rude, look, I need your support.

They were sent over a week ago, they looked desperate too. But I haven't got the energy at the moment. I haven't even been going to work, never mind anything else. Can't be bothered with any of my messages or the outside world for that matter. I switch off my phone and throw it back into my handbag. I sigh, as I look over at my laptop. I'm not in the right frame of mind to do anything. Even my dreams aren't tormenting me here.

* * *

At a stand-still in the jungle; hazy, suffocating atmosphere; unable to move forward; stood outside the bank I take a deep breath and push open the door.

'Here she is,' Carol shouts. 'Have you lost weight Lucy?'

'I don't think so; I'm not sure.'

'Jenny's got me doing your job as well as my own; looking after leaflets and everything. Is that okay with you or should I stop, now you're back?'

'No, you carry on, and to be honest Carol, all this leaflet business is nonsense; a made-up job, to make it look like I was being given extra responsibility. It's not being worked like this in any of the other branches, but I just went along with it; got used to it I suppose,' I say, as I input the security code on the door that leads to the stairs.

'Hello Lucy,' Jenny says, with a beaming smile as I walk into her office.

'Hello,' I say, as I sit down and face her; really don't want to be sat in this sinking atmosphere.

'How are you feeling Lucy?'

'Fine, thanks; really well, actually.'

'Good, well I'll let you get on with it then. Don't worry about the leaflets and all that. Carol's really keen to develop, so if it's okay with you I'm letting her manage those.'

'That's fine with me,' I say, smirking and feeling highly amused.

'Well, you know where I am if you need anything,' Jenny says with a smile, and looks at her computer screen.

Stand up and walk towards the door. So relieved to get out of that room and walk down the stairs; don't care that Jenny is completely unsupportive.

* * *

In dimming daylight, I hesitantly walk to Victoria's house; look towards the glorious, blood-orange glow of the sunset. Even though I don't know what to expect, it sure feels better than walking home, knowing exactly what to expect there.

Nervously open the front gate and walk up the pathway to her house. Ring the bell and live in hope that she's not in; but the gleaming, four-wheel drive is a giveaway that she is at home.

'Hi Lucy,' Victoria says, with a welcoming smile as she opens her door. Looking picture-perfect as her jet-black, sculptured, chic, bobbed hair shines solidly. Her large, brown eyes sparkle behind her black, square-framed glasses.

'Hello Victoria.'

'Come in. You've come at a good time; my mum's just taken the children to hers until tomorrow,' Victoria gushes.

Wide, open hallway; original, multi-coloured, tiled floor. Polished mahogany, spindled staircase; stairs dressed with pure-red, plush carpet.

'Sit down in here. I'll get us a glass of red wine,' Victoria says, as she opens a door to the right of the hallway and ushers me in. 'Make yourself at home.'

I sit down on the plush, white, leather settee. I take off my shoes when I notice the pure-white, carpeted flooring.

'There you go,' Victoria says, as she hands me a glass of red wine.

'I'm sorry I never replied to your texts; I only read them a week after they'd been sent. I didn't want to speak to anyone to be honest,' I say.

'Don't worry. Rick told me you were off sick. He was worried about you as you're never off work!'

'This wine's nice,' I say, as I sip.

'It's my favourite, but I don't drink much since having the children. So like I say, you've come at the right time. We can have a proper catch-up.'

I just smile; she certainly doesn't seem to have anything against me; nothing like what Carol was on about.

'I texted you to let you know that Rick had left his phone here. I could see that you'd been speaking quite a bit recently. But, don't worry; I know about the Rick and Andy thing,' Victoria announces, in a matter-of-fact way.

Feeling uncomfortable as I sip my wine.

'It came to a head just before I sent you those texts. Sorry to say it, but you and Rick did cross my mind. I think it was just because I was at my worst; common sense was telling me nothing was going on, but you know what they say about common sense going out of the window. I was going to storm into the bank to confront you, and I told Rick I knew he was holding back on something. He sat me down and started to tell me the truth about what had been going on. I'll get us another glass of wine,' Victoria says, as she takes my glass out of my hand and walks out of the room.

Pounding heart, drumming its way into my throat; tightening chest as I try to breathe calmly; uncomfortable and unsure how I should react; hoping 'Project Sandwich' doesn't come up and I need to decide whether to be honest if she mentions it.

'There you go,' Victoria says, as she passes me another glass of red wine.

'What were you saying about Rick and Andy,' I ask; unsure if I'm meant to know or not.

'So, you don't know?' Victoria asks.

'I know that they're mates from school, and they meet for lunch.' At least I've not lied; I've just not told her all of the detail.

'I'd best bring the other bottle in before I tell you; you'll need it,' Victoria says, as she gets up and walks out of the room.

Guilt-ridden, rising body temperature. I feel sorry for her; she's being supportive towards me before she tells me what I already know.

'Rick and I have been having problems for a long time.' Victoria exclaims, as she walks into the room and sits next to me, slamming the bottle of wine down onto the coffee table. 'Looking back, the 'marriage and babies' thing happened too quickly. The fun went out of our relationship. One minute I was Vicky Bates and the next I was Victoria Black, the wife of a bank manager. I thought I had to stop having fun to be a good wife; I took things too seriously. The excitement went out of our sex life too, probably because Rick was stressed at work. Missionary position for five minutes is nothing to get excited about is it? Especially when it's a hot night and Rebecca had me up the night before. I don't know ... Rick and I stopped talking and I knew there was something wrong. I was always too tired for sex after I gave birth to Rebecca. Well, when I was pregnant too; so I always compensated by giving Rick oral. At least it gave him a bit of relief. But he never wanted me near it, so I knew it must have been somewhere it shouldn't have,' Victoria sighs.

I carry on sipping my wine; I don't want to break Victoria's rhythm of chat, and she needs to get it out.

'I never thought it would be Andy. I obviously never thought it would be you, as I know how straight you are. But I was clutching at straws out of sheer frustration. Apparently, they only had full, penetrable sex once, and he used a condom. I wouldn't mind but he's not even gay,' Victoria sighs, and wipes a tear from her cheek.

'Rick started going to Andy's for a couple of drinks, which I knew about. I wasn't drinking with being pregnant, so I didn't mind that. Rick said he fell asleep as he'd had a few too many, and it first started when he was awoken by Andy caressing him. He said he was a bit disorientated at first but felt aroused. It doesn't take much does it? He knew deep-down that he wasn't gay; he said it was an escape.'

'I don't know what to say Victoria.'

'Neither do I Lucy. Rick had the nerve to say he wanted us to work things out. How can I?' Victoria continues.

'What are you going to do?'

'Well, I don't want to make any rash decisions like divorce, but I want to be left alone for a while. I need time to think; do I throw away a marriage and relationship I've been in for years because of a mad, lurid, two-month period Rick had? He's renting an apartment in Liverpool so he's giving me loads of space. I do still love him; I know that, but I'm not sure if I can forgive him. To be honest, I'm myself more now, so you can stop calling me Victoria,' she laughs.

'Thank God for that. I had to remember not to call you Vicky whenever I said your name,' I laugh.

'I don't know who I thought I was. I cringe with embarrassment. I suppose I was hiding what I was really feeling to be honest. I've not been happy for a long time, but don't worry, I won't get you drunk and make a pass at you,' Vicky laughs.

'Stop it; you're making me worry now,' I laugh.

'My mum has the children one night a week, which is brilliant, and Rick has them every Friday night, so I've got it made really. I'm going to sell the house though. I want to live near my mum; most of my mates are there too. Rick was so relieved; I mean this house was out of our reach anyway; it was just a status symbol. The relief on Rick's face was a picture. We should make about £100,000 on this, so Rick said I can have that towards my next house. The houses near my mum are only about £150,000 so that'll do me. It'll be in my name; my mortgage, so I'm actually feeling good about myself,' Vicky continues.

'You certainly look good after having William.'

'Thanks Lucy; it's only been four weeks, but I've been under a lot of stress, so I guess that's helped. That's why my mum's chipped in with babysitting; she said I need to rest. I don't know what I'd do without her,' Vicky says, as she smiles to herself and sips her wine.

* * *

Disheartened; self-pitying as I walk home. Don't get me wrong, I am pleased for Vicky and really glad she's managed to keep herself together. She's actually improving her life and finding peace within the carnage. I suppose I'm disheartened because of my own life.

Chapter 6

My pitiful heart used to skip to a flamboyant beat, feel as free as a bird … but that feeling no longer exists; tortured, it is deeply burdened, a burden I can no longer carry, weighted down. It now sinks deep and carries my soul with it, as I walk through the front door after another hard day at work. They jump downwards, like two small children holding hands as they jump into the deep end of a swimming pool for the first time. Mike's need completely engulfs me as I gasp for breath and walk into the kitchen. Emotionally knocked off my feet as a roaring wind thunders around. Mike is marching heavy-footed as I'm transfixed to the spot. No longer safe; he's found me again.

'You'll never get rid of me. I thought I made that clear to you from the beginning.'

Tearfully look back towards my field at the cliff's edge. Dullness of the early-evening sky against the darkened outline of the cliff's edge reminds me I'll never be able to reach it again! It now represents bleakness in the distance as I yearn for the feeling of long, soft grass against my skin. I have to stay here and face Mike. A feeling of defeated exhaustion fills me from the pit of my stomach and is rising upwards. How do I stop this from dragging me down into another bout of illness? If I let it take hold, I'll be off work again and I'll sleep for up to twenty hours a day, for days that lead to weeks. I have to pull myself out of my vicious circle.

I yearn to live in ignorance of it for a few seconds longer. Staring out at nothing, desperately trying to block him out of my existence; he's in my face again, poking me. The continuous poking irritates me so much. I know I'm enabling him but he'll continue to hit me over the head with his emotional hammer, until I give him my seal of approval. He needs that from me; he wants it all.

Desperately look out towards the sixth island, hoping for a vision, a helping-hand, but I can't see it anymore. No longer in my sight, Mike continues his emotional battering, and he is creating a cloud of dust as he continues to thunder around; billowing up as each foot pounds onto the dry, grainy floor; stamping around like a determined child. I can't stand listening to him but he wants to be heard; he wants his demands taken care of. Mike grabs hold as I try to move back towards the safety of the jungle, catching a glimpse of a Perspex bubble as it bobs up and down in the swamp water. Fear is sitting inside, beckoning me towards it; to join it, so I can hide away. But Mike's shaking me out of my daze and the bubble starts to drift away. Mike wants me to focus on him, but I can't any more. He's towering over me with his hands on my shoulders; he doesn't know what to do; he can't get through to me. His frustration rises in his face and he propels me backwards, pushing me away as he lets go and storms off. I can feel my body falling ... floating ... in mid-air. A sense of landing softly overcomes me, as Fear takes hold and softens my fall; and now it has me in its grasp as we float away.

Crying ... it's safe to cry ... I'm stranded with Fear inside my bubble as it gently bobs up and down in the swamp water. Pleading, wishing I was dead ... emotionally victimised as I hold onto Fear, with its strong arms wrapped around me as I drift away ... away from this crazy world. Crying myself to sleep. Child-like feelings within the soothing motion of drifting on the gentle current of water.

* * *

Wetness on my face is the first sensation I feel; awareness of the feeling within my hair and underneath my body. The wetness seems to be on my left side only. I can feel grainy, hard particles in my right hand and underneath that arm. Sensing the coldness around me, within me, as I gasp for breath, I move my right hand and feel for the grainy particles. Light filters onto my face; I can sense that, even with my eyes closed. Wetness glides underneath my body and imperceptibly lifts me from the place in which I am lying. Wetness then leaves me; a sensation of draining away as my body falls flat back into place. Cold shivers through my body as the wetness drains away and I wait for it to glide beneath me again. Desire to be as I am ... to remain ... no real movement or emotion, or even life.

As everyone's life is moving on, I'm still stuck on the fifth island, unable to move forward. My confidence has gone; I feel worthless, sad and old beyond my years.

Open my eyes but unsure if I am actually *seeing* ... not trusting that I am still in denial and living in ignorance of it all. Making it easy for myself; shutting myself away. I sit up, unable to cope with the coldness any longer. The left side of my body is actually lying in the swamp water with only my right side touching the island. With no sign of my bubble, Fear or Mike, I can breathe. Feeling unsafe I look back towards the middle of the island; the trunk of the large tree is exposed on this side. It is flourishing; sitting proud like the grandfather of all trees, with exposed roots that have created areas of shelter. They reach upwards from underneath the earth. I crawl towards them and nestle myself within the huge, bulking roots. The trunk is covered with a layer of green and orange-coloured moss. Small tufts of grass sporadically sprout out, and new shoots of jungle branches entwine themselves around the trunk. Quivering in the coldness, I huddle myself against the velvet feel of the moss and look out towards the sixth island. A breath-taking view, deep-orange sun settled behind jungle trees, as alive as a deep-seated fire as it reflects across swamp waters.

Melanie and I are not meeting each day, as Paul is working in the gardens. The council have finally moved the sandwich van and are revamping the place, reopening in four weeks for a carnival. I told Melanie to spend the next four weeks with Paul and we can meet again after that; said I didn't mind; I had a few things to do. The truth is, I've gone into myself; in no mood for small talk. I prefer to go deep inside and think things through in my head or try to block it out; carry on as best I can. Completely weighed down, it's exhausting; as if a sack of coal is being placed onto my shoulders and I can't put it down anywhere, so I just carry it around all day and night.

Mike drinks until he passes out; it makes me feel physically agitated, listening to the same drunken drivel every night; I can't stand it any longer. Sick to death of the constant tricks he seems to have up his sleeve. Excuses to get me to the shops when he runs out of money. Electrical appliances seem to mysteriously break down, the kettle, the toaster, even the fridge. A fake burst of energy to give up smoking; it's okay to drink every night then? A DIY frenzy. Promises he can't keep, just to get me out of the house to start looking for a new kitchen or sofa. Then it's time for a drink. No energy to move forward, I sit, clinging to the same jungle tree. I'm stuck and struggle to wake up each morning. No longer watch the sunrise; the sun hasn't warmed my face for a while.

As daylight touches my face and early-morning dew soaks my skin, I let go of the jungle tree. Back to the robotic work mode of a zone filled with smog and haze, I look up at the door that leads into the bank where I work. The door is sodden, rotting-wood which crumbles when touched. A creaking, fragile entrance that has a time limit; soaked to the skin, trembling in this dream-like atmosphere, I step over the bulky roots and delicately open the door. Trudging into work, not wanting to communicate with others and zoning myself out as best I can; I work hard all day, it takes my mind off things. Step out of work and cling onto my tree; hide myself between the bulky roots. The jungle has turned into a dark place again. The wind has picked up, so I use the rope-like branches to tie myself to the trunk, to make sure I'm safe and secure. No longer sleeping; don't know how I'm surviving, but I am. Sitting at the foot of the tree, staring at the sixth island and I stay there until it's time to untie myself and walk into work again. In darkness and exposed to the dry, gritty wind; feels like sandpaper against my face and body. Staring at the sixth island, playing with the grainy soil; small particles run through my fingers and back onto the floor of the island. I just about have the energy to get up and walk through the door, into work. Much later in the day, I try to leave but realise the doorway has moved; panic as I look around and realise everyone has left for the day. The only light is filtering in from the dim streetlights. Jungle branches hang down from the ceiling. Frightened and clinging onto a rope-like branch, I look up to see a doorway fixed to the ceiling. Too scared to let go, I drag a chair across the floor, place it directly underneath the doorway. Sitting on the chair, clinging onto my branch and staring at the ceiling ... thinking; unsure if I can reach, I stand up on the chair. Not sure how I'm going to climb up; was never any good at rope-climbing in PE at school, and I'm nowhere near as nimble as I was then, and I weigh a lot more. I throw my heavy handbag onto the floor, take off my coat and throw that on the floor too. Twist the rope and pull myself up, so that the end of the rope is wrapped around my ankle. Weakened; upper-body strength being pushed to the limit as I continue to pull myself upwards and as I near the doorway, I grab hold of a looped branch and kneel upon it. Rest my body for a minute then stand on the loop; like standing on the seat of a swing, I am unsteady but pull myself up onto the door frame. Peering into the jungle; the door has collapsed onto the floor of the island; rotting hinges torn away from the jungle tree. Using twine to pull myself onto the floor of the island; tie myself to the trunk. Feeling exposed as a low wind swirls across the waters, preventing me from seeing the sixth island. Sinking heart as I realise it may be lost forever and, knowing it's my fault, I've resigned myself to this life.

Self-pity smothers the air in this smog of existence with no sense of reality; huddling down within the bulky roots of the trunk. No choice but to sit awake all night again, there's no sleep within me tonight. Not feeling or seeing anything real, I don't bother to untie myself and go to work. Settled into this place with its velvet feel of comfort; emotionally imprisoned. I can hear Mike mimic me as he realises I'm not well again. Fear is huddled next to me, submerged and preventing me from reaching out for help.

Mike's on the edge, sat at the edge of the island, next to the water, looking up at me with poisonous eyes, keeping guard. Strangled by fear; I am going to die here, in this place. Instant realisation reaches my existence as I look at him. I believe in what Fear is telling me. Maybe Fear has been more of a friend to me than I realise, letting me know how I am feeling inside. Mike relies on me for everything in his life, and I am realising that I can no longer move with his weight and burden on my back. I cannot make another person happy; they have to make themselves happy. Look at Mike, knowing I don't love him anymore and know, *really know* that I do have a choice, even though he says I don't. Not causing alcoholism; knowing I will never change it and certainly do not have a cure, I am powerless. I need to focus on myself instead of his next drink. Mike looks stunned as I stand up and firmly-press my back against the velvet feel of the tree trunk. He doesn't know what to do; he doesn't know what his next manipulation is going to be.

Unable to go to work, I have to deal with this now. Uncontrollable pleading and continual, exhausting cries, as Mike begs for another chance. With nothing left to give, he can't wear me down anymore. He tugs at my empty shell of a body. I feel nothing. No longer frightened by his invasion of my space, I can focus on me and me alone. It's as if his power and manipulation is diminishing in this atmosphere, as mine is getting stronger. Fear has broken what has now become the not-so-vicious circle. With both hands against my chest, I can breathe; lurching forward as I gasp for deep breaths, Fear knows I'm ready to face this somehow. Amazing relief surges through me as the strangle-hold is removed.

'But I love you,' Mike shouts, in frustration.

No longer arguing with the bottle, there's no point and I no longer add to the problem. Though I am struggling to detach with kindness, I would rather not look at him and not listen to him at all.

'You're a fucking fool if you let me go! No one will love you like I do. Are you listening to me?'

I am listening but I'm not reacting; just stare out, past him, though realising I definitely have a choice now. I don't have the energy for him; save my energy for myself.

Catch a glimpse as the mist melts away from the stream of water to reveal the sixth island in all its beauty. Step forward to the edge of the stream and the grey of the large stepping-stones that protrude from the water. Sunlight captures the greenness of the foliage that climbs the thin trunks of the tall jungle trees, in contrast to the nakedness of some bare trees. Misty sky hangs in the distance. Knowing I need to move, I step onto the first of the firm, grey rock stepping stones, making sure my right foot feels supported before I lift my left from the island. Feeling secure, carefully treading along the steps to reach the sixth island.

I have an invisible barrier of protection forming around me as I try to move forward in my life. I can't look at Mike in too much detail as I'd fall back into my vicious circle. His frustration has dampened, and he is slowly coming to terms with the situation. He sits in deep thought at times and I see his face fall. He can't believe it. He can't believe that I am going through with this and will see it through to the end. I can't believe it myself either, but I have to do this; I have to think of me. Constantly remind myself to concentrate on me, and my inner self.

Chapter 7

Threats of violence, manipulation and control overwhelm me at times, but feelings of emptiness help me to detach. Realising I do have a choice, watching it all unfold without reacting, sheds new light on Mike's cowardly behaviour. Knowing that physical rest is what I need to help me tackle this to the end. I decide to take the plunge and go on holiday on my own. John is on his annual holiday with his best friend and his family, so it's now or never.

An absolute need to be by myself, to rest my emotions; the thought of sitting on the beach reading a good book sounds like heaven to me. Not caring about my house anymore and the threats of what Mike will do whilst I'm gone. Burn it down if you have to. Placing the dog with a friend, I feel happy as I drive to the airport and park up in the long stay carpark. An aura of escapism as I wheel my suitcase through the entrance doors of the airport terminal, analysing the screens for my holiday agency; need to make sure I stand in the correct queue. Purposely not looking at those who are stood around me or even listening to their conversations.

Craving peace, I just want to remain calm. Place my suitcase on the weighing scale and watch it glide away to be placed into the hold of the plane; my tickets are returned to me by the smiling travel agent.

Passing security is a breeze; reaching for the large plastic carton that contains my hand bag, shoes, coat and belt. Put my shoes back on and the strap of my handbag over my shoulder, then fold my coat over my left arm. Zoning everything out; I must be nervous. Immense desire to be left alone; purposely look at the floor then find a seat and allow the hours to pass whilst I wait to board my plane.

I don't feel a pang of nervousness as I board the plane for a five-hour flight; smile with relief knowing I am being taken away, taken out of this atmosphere and into another world for a few days.

* * *

The holiday rep is waiting with his clipboard as I walk towards the exit doors of the airport in the foreign land. He guides me to the coach that will take me to my all-inclusive accommodation, a great, last-minute deal.

Stepping off the coach gives me a sense of real freedom. Tropical heat, welcoming warmth against my skin and a real smile emerges. Relieved I stand back as the coach driver pulls my suitcase from the hold and places it on the floor at my feet.

Looking towards the hotel, grey-coloured, paved steps lead upwards towards the vast, glassed, double entrance doors. Metal railings on either side of the steps, and a concrete ramp for wheelchair access. Beautiful gardens and foliage outline either side. The driveway to the hotel is inviting; huge, flower-emblazoned roundabout is the turning point for vehicles when dropping holidaymakers off at the entrance. Marble sign with the name of the hotel picked out with lights and a huge water feature sit in the centre. Watching as the coach steers around the turning-point and exits the hotel driveway. I laugh as I look back towards the hotel; can't quite believe I'm here. Got more guts than I thought. Hold onto the rail and lug my suitcase up the steps. Wheel my suitcase across the golden-coloured, marble floor, as I approach the expansive reception desk. Stand and wait to be served, watching the smiling receptionists. There are three of them, two male and one female; they look like triplets with identical, crisp, short-sleeved, white shirts emblazoned with the hotel logo. With perfect, olive skin, jet-black, shiny hair and beautiful, deep-brown eyes. Name tags confirm their names are Veronica, Laurence and Antoine. They smile and are welcoming, and Veronica invites me to get a drink and something to eat before the lunchtime bar closes. She ties my all-inclusive wristband to my wrist, passes me my room keys and a card with printed directions to my room, situated within the large complex. I leave my suitcase in reception and take a deep breath as I walk outside and sit by the pool with a glass of apple juice and some fries. The white, plastic tables are littered with cocktail glasses filled with bright liquid, paper umbrellas and straws. Half-empty pint-glasses and small plates of half-eaten food; the pool is filled with happy faces, laughter, and the air is filled with screeches of joy, crappy-music and a male voice talking into a microphone. The holiday rep is clambering round, trying to encourage everyone to join in a darts competition. I look down towards my drink as he whizzes past me in his hyperactivity, voice screeching, catching a glimpse of his startling-yellow shirt. Realising I need to be alone and at peace, I leave my half-eaten fries and half-empty glass of apple juice and walk back towards reception to collect my suitcase.

I'm greeted by the manager of the hotel; no name on the manager tag that is pinned onto his crisp-white shirt, but he has the most beautiful, smiley face I have ever seen. A strikingly handsome black man. Eyebrows arch upwards in the centre; an archway to heaven as far as I am concerned. Dream-like eyes; deep-brown, perfect, they ooze sensuality and are the absolute focal point. Transfixed and hypnotised by his amazing face. Strong, outstanding cheekbones contour his face from the outer side of each eye and firmly slice down towards his full lips which have just broken out into the most endearing smile. He wants to wheel my suitcase to my room, even though I have no problem doing this myself. Embarrassingly we both reach for the handle and wheel it across the marble floor, through the automatic, glass doors and down the ramp. Warm, tropical air touches my face and soothes my soul as we walk along, not talking but feeling comfortable and safe. A block-paved, tree-lined pathway with immaculately cut, thick blades of deep-green grass on either side; tall trees with trunks that look like cracked, brown leather and two-tone in colour; green and yellow palms high above swishing in the soothing, warm wind. Glancing at the directions on the card; dismissing the fact that *he* is with me. The door to my room is open and the cleaning lady leaves with a smile. My basic, clean room feels welcoming; cream-coloured tiles on the floor, dark-coloured, wooden double bed with high headboard and high end. Two dark-coloured, wooden, bedside tables with a lamp on each; small, wooden dressing-table and two-door wardrobe also made with the same dark wood. Terracotta bedcovers and matching curtains which are tied back, either side of the sliding glass doors which lead to a large balcony. I put my suitcase on the bed and walk towards the glass doors, slide them open and walk onto the balcony and look out onto the beach. Expansive, sandy beach; sand looks whiter as it nears the turquoise sea. Palm trees outline the entrance to the hotel. Rows of sunbeds and umbrellas lay near the beach bar. Piles of black rocks make the beach look dirty in places. A volcano towers in the distance. Realising *he* is no longer with me and feeling a bit ignorant for not noticing, I walk back into the room and open my suitcase. Immediately get changed into my bikini, t-shirt and shorts, pull out the bottle of sun-cream and apply it to the exposed parts of my body. Loading my beach bag with sun-cream, a book, purse, keys, sunglasses, and mobile phone, I leave my room and walk towards the beach. Not feeling lonely as I walk past families and other groups of people, relieved to be on my own.

Sinking deep into the mounds of fine, warm sand, I remove my sandals; walk bare foot towards the sunbeds. I remove my t-shirt and shorts and lie on a lounger as the heat of the sun instantly makes me feel sleepy. I leave my book in my bag and lie on my back closing my eyes, careful to check the time on my phone so I don't lie here for too long. I don't want to get sunburnt on my first day.

The tightness on my face wakes me from my sleep; panic a little but when I check the time on my phone, I've only been lying here for an hour. I turn over realising I haven't got anyone to put sun-cream on my back. I struggle to do this myself, but it seems impossible. Looking across to the hotel in frustration, I laugh inside as I realise the manager is making his way over to me. Surely this isn't in his job description.

'Do you want me to put some sun-cream on your back?' the lady on the next sunbed shouts over.

'That would be great.'

She sits to place her bikini straps on her shoulders. Wearing a black bikini, she must be in her mid-forties with a toned figure. Large sunglasses cover most of her face and the searing sun prevents me from getting a clear look at her features. But she does have long-layered, wavy, deep-brown hair. I reach for my sun-cream as she ties her hair back with an elastic hair-tie. She takes the bottle of sun-cream out of my hand, and I tilt my head up as the manager walks past; he probably wasn't coming my way anyway; maybe it's my mind, playing games with me as usual. Intense coldness on my back distracts me as she squirts the sun-cream, and then gently rubs it in with her hand.

'Thanks a lot,' I say, as she finishes applying the cream.

'No problem,' she answers, as she passes me the bottle and lies back down on her sunbed.

Reaching inside my bag for five euro, I hold it up to where a man is standing. Not having the energy to look at him, he removes the five euro from my hand and puts a ticket in its place. Well at least that's my sunbed sorted for the day. My head falls heavily onto the sunbed. I'm wanting to be left alone now; needing a blank mind to rest and sleep for a while.

Melting in the intense heat, look up to make sure my large umbrella is helping to shade my body. Feeling bored, I decide to go for a walk along the beach. I put on my shorts; lay my towel over the sunbed so no one else sits there. Leave my sandals underneath, pick up my bag and walk towards the sea. Warm, fine sand particles scrub my feet as they sink with every step. My feet remain on the surface of the wet, darkened sand; turquoise waves, edged with whiteness lap towards me as the sea cools my lower legs. Feels like paradise as I walk along the shoreline and towards the quiet emptiness of the far end of the beach. Away from noise and crowds of people, I'm in a different world. Look out at the expanse of blue sea, as blue as the sky. No differentiation between the sea and the sky until the sea glistens like glass as the sun sweeps across it. Free mind and spirit; smiling as nakedness approaches. Nudists running into the sea as I reach my turning point, which is a pile of rocks in the sand. I turn around, to walk back to my sunbed; I can see him in the distance, like a black knight guarding his fortress. As I get nearer to my sunbed, he turns and walks back into the grounds of the hotel.

Smiling as I stand at the beach bar, I give two euro for a bottle of water, then lie down on my sunbed, sipping slowly while reaching into my bag for my book. Relax and read in the safe, warm environment.

* * *

The clouds have darkened the sky as I walk back towards the hotel and the deep sand has cooled in the early evening air. Near-empty beach, large umbrellas being tied, shutters locked on the beach bar. My mind feels empty and clear as I walk through the gate and into the grounds of the hotel complex. I use the wash area to remove the sand from my feet. Dry them with a towel, put on my sandals then walk to my room along the block-paved pathway. Tightness in my face from too much sun, but warmth in my heart; restfulness; trying to live in *today*.

Opening the door to my room, it smells fresh and clean; empty, darkened room but no loneliness, just an appreciation of it. Examine my reddened face, tight skin and smudged mascara as I look in the mirror that's fixed to the wall. I get showered and wash my hair. Sitting down, I dry and straighten my hair and put on my makeup. Excited as I pull out a new dress from my suitcase; I bought it specially for my holiday; electric-blue, knee-length, strapless, fitted and then slightly floats out from the waist. Brown leather belt to cinchin the waist, and matching brown leather, wedge-heeled sandals.

* * *

After eating my late evening meal, I walk into the bar to the sound of the evening entertainment. A waiter leads me to a candle-lit table decorated with simple, fresh flowers sat in a pure-white, porcelain holder.

Warm feeling rises within my cheeks as I notice the black knight sat alone at a table to the left of mine. He's not looking over as I glimpse him; admiring his bulging physique, plain, dark, navy-blue trousers and white, fitted shirt.

Melting heart as he looks over; I smile meekly and turn away to look towards the stage. The barmen try to make my apple juice appear more exciting by adding different coloured straws, umbrellas and sparklers, exploding light out into the room.

Feeling secure and knowing that someone is obviously looking after me during this stay. Wanting an early start tomorrow, I get up to leave and one of the barmen follows me out of the room and asks me to go to reception. I do as he asks and one of the receptionists leads me outside to what looks like a golf buggy. Offering to take me back to my room, I sit next to Antoine. The buggy picks up speed against the refreshing breeze as it trundles along the scenic route; the path that runs alongside the beach. A breath-taking view as the moonlit sea thunders in the distance. Politely thank Antoine as I step off the buggy and enter my room.

* * *

Wake up refreshed and relieved, knowing I am actually on holiday, on my own and this isn't one of my silly dreams. Step out of bed and walk out onto the balcony; the beach is an amazing sight. Smile with excitement at the thought of spending the day out there. No time wasted as I get ready and head out for breakfast.

Refreshingly-warm sea, rushing waves pushing against me, then pushing me back to shore. Surrounded by laughter, as holidaymakers have fun in the high waves, I'm careful to keep my feet on the ground as my body merges deeper into the turquoise water. Body boards and lilos seem far out at sea, until the waves push them back towards the shore.

Trudging back to the shore with water at chest height, a force hits me from behind. Knocked under water, I can feel it push me, but I'm struggling to get back to my feet. Panic-stricken, I feel a strong pair of hands pull me out and carry me to the shore. Stinging eyes, I dry them with a towel as I take a look at my rescuer, and I'm relieved to see that it's one of the life-guards. Sip on my water to wash the disgusting saltiness away. An apologetic, distraught man stands next to me, holding on to his body board. Smile in appreciation as I sit and sip water.

A surge of invisible energy and then the black knight arrives and sits next to me. Internally melting away within his presence as I fit neatly into his frame, he places both arms around me and rubs my back with a large, luxurious towel. Not wanting to change the dynamics of this moment, quietly sitting ever so still, when all I want to do is melt my head into his chest. This is just a moment of reassurance and comfort on his part. I suppose I'm the damsel in distress. I know ... another sick-bucket moment.

A sudden emptiness: breathless emotion as he stands and walks away. Surreal moment as I watch his body of steel. Every inch is pure, physical pleasure and he moves so masterfully back to the hotel.

* * *

A beautiful sunset sets the sky on fire like a magnificent, beaming torch. A skyline of pure-orange haze shadows the entire atmosphere as we lie in each other's arms. Muscular arms, a force of energy, tightly wrapped around me; soft, delicate embrace as his lips caress my neck and shoulders. Shivers delicately tingle down my spine; an intense sensation that brings my body back to life. Tightness in his hold upon my body; too intense, no longer able to resist. I am resuscitated into another dimension, and I turn to face him, to be moulded into his body. Lips that want to surrender in this moment. A body that yearns for the warmth of his body, captivated by his hold; crave to have this feeling forever.

Smiling. A true smile of relief as I wake from my desire-drenched dreams.

* * *

Standing at the gate that leads to the beach from the hotel, his gleaming smile touches mine and I know I have nowhere to hide. He's wearing light-coloured, cotton trousers and short-sleeved, loose shirt that couldn't possibly hide those muscular arms. A hotel waiter walks towards us and passes a small cool box. Puzzled, I smile as we both hold the handle. We stroll together without saying a word. I can't help but breathe in the beauty of the idyllic beach. Breath-taking, turquoise sea and pure-white sand. He stops and looks out towards the sea; I stand with him and admire different shades of blue.

'It's beautiful, isn't it?' he says, as we admire the view.

'It certainly is.'

'I was born here, and I've stepped onto this beach every day of my life. Who needs to escape when they have this?'

'I agree, you truly are lucky to experience this every day.'

'Come on,' he says, as he walks ahead towards the sand dunes.

I follow him and we start to walk up the dunes towards a large palm tree. There's a semi-circular rock wall about one metre high to help shelter from the wind.

'The nudists normally use these shelters, but the locals know that this is my spot, so no-one comes here, except me. I just love this place; it looks like a mini island with the huge palm tree and spectacular views.'

I open the cool-box; one bottle of ice-cold water and two containers of food, a mixed-leaf salad and seafood rice dish. I look into his eyes as he shakes his head, not wanting any food, I spoon the seafood rice into a wooden bowl and eat. Sit in silence and look out to sea. Sweeping sea-breeze, cooling our bodies.

'So, tell me, why are you so sad?'

I'm too shocked to answer at first. I'm not sure if I feel like opening up to someone I don't really know, but on the other hand, it's not as if I'm going to see him again after this holiday.

'My life has become unmanageable,' I reply.

'In what way?'

'Well, I'm not too sure. My relationship with my husband, Mike, has failed; let's just say his personal, life-style choices have made me feel really unhappy for the last few years. I have been trying to face up to the fact I'm not happy and need to move forward without him in my life.'

'What do you do to enjoy life?' he asks.

I pause for a while, struggling to think of anything. 'I don't seem to enjoy anything at the moment.'

'You need to find a way to resolve this, but you won't be able to, unless you start looking at yourself first, one day at a time. Think about it. I'll leave you with that thought; there is a way. Take care of you, the rest will follow,' he says, as he stands up to leave and walks back towards the hotel.

'Take care of me', I say to myself, as I watch him walk away.

* * *

Sigh, as I pack the rest of my belongings into my suitcase. Admire my tan in the long mirror that's fixed to the wall, next to my bed. A real smile plastered onto my tanned face. A worrying wince as I realise I haven't seen anything of the hotel manager since our little talk by the sea. I hope I didn't freak him out. Listen to me, I think too much sometimes. As if the 'opening up police' will come to arrest me.

As I check out of the hotel, Veronica cuts the all-inclusive band from my wrist. It's then I notice a large portrait of the man of steel. There's a plaque underneath the portrait, but I can't make out what it says.

'Who is that in the portrait and what does the plaque say?'

'That's Adetokunbo. We called him Ade for short and he was named after the sea; the crown of the sea. But it was the sea that took him away,' she replies, in broken English.

'What do you mean?'

'Sadly, he died four years ago; he drowned trying to rescue a holidaymaker. Very sad time, very sad now. We miss him every single day. He was a very strong swimmer, so we can only think that he was needed in heaven,' she continues.

'But ... but, I saw him. I've spoken to him during my holiday,' I stammer, in complete shock.

'Well, if you did, then you are very lucky. It seems somebody sees him as each year passes. You must be special in some way, so if you learnt something from him, take it home with you and use it,' she says, in a matter-of-fact way and then goes to serve the next person.

Numbingly shocked as I walk outside, wheeling my suitcase behind me and sit on the bench as I wait for the coach.

Whizzing mind as I obsess about my time with Ade. What about the time he wheeled my suitcase; the time he was sat on a table next to me and the time he comforted me when I nearly drowned. What about the time he walked towards me when I couldn't put sun cream on my back and spent time sat with me by the sea?

Look out towards the sea as the coach drives out of the driveway of the hotel and along the coast road. No sign of him, and when I think about the times I have seen him, no one else seems to have. No one has spoken to him, and the only time he spoke to me was when we were alone.

* * *

Look out of the small window on the plane: the wide-open space of the sky is beautifully peaceful. Absolute freedom makes me realise that we should all feel free. But I also realise that it can be taken away at any time if we don't look after our freedom. I have to look after *me* now, one day at a time, and I keep that thought with me as I drive home from the airport.

With Ade's words in my head, I start to look at myself and the part I have played in my life. I can't blame everything on Mike. I accepted the life we had and I wanted to make him happy; look after him regardless. I became completely obsessed with his drinking instead of looking after my own life.

Focusing on, and living my own life, Mike and I start to get along a lot better; there's a mutual respect and I start to see the good things again. I don't feel responsible for him or his behaviour. Have I remained detached? My determination and natural feeling to part stays with me and has finally paid off, Mike is moving out at the end of the week.

It feels surreal as I stumble through the waters towards the seventh island, like my life before now was not mine. Coldness within the shallow water stings my feet and lower legs as I slowly move. Bright dots of light, surrounded by hypnotic beams, confused until I look towards the seventh island. Light, shining out from behind the density of the foliage; fixated by the light as it shines onto my body, like reflections from a disco ball. Treading in sluggish swamp bed as I near the island; a dream-like atmosphere as light spears from between the gaps in the foliage and jungle trees, familiar feel of the sticky fern scraping against my legs as I try to walk through it. Holding onto the thin, gangly branches of the jungle trees and gingerly stepping over foliage and bracken, being careful not to stumble. Drawn towards the blinding light that's searing through the near-impossible entanglement of the foliage that is twisting around the trees. Not equipped with the tools I need, knowing I need help and realising that asking is not a form of weakness. Not asking and being the martyr is the real weakness.

As night falls, I walk into a large clearing on the island. Thick, tangled fern tugging at my waist, knowing I may have to use the fern as shelter tonight. Naked trees growing tall and close together, standing to attention, as smooth as cane. My physical and mental energy is quite strong when Mike is coping with the idea of moving out, but as soon as he can't cope with it, I can't move; he squeezes at my heart and drains the life out of it. When he agreed to move out, I spent a good few hours pottering in the garden and I recognised myself for a while, like being with an old friend. It can be zapped out of me in an instant though and I don't like that, so the sooner this is resolved, the sooner I can get back to work.

* * *

I feel quite robotic as the move-out date arrives and I help move Mike's belongings into his flat; try to support without taking over. I don't feel anything; genuinely feel nothing.

Chapter 8

There is freedom and lightness in each step as I walk down the High Street towards work. I have an awareness and clarity of mind, as I look up into the sky; a sky that is pale-blue and slightly clouded with gentle whiteness. Occupied with a smile that is real; acknowledgement that I am here in this moment, here with all of my mind and heart. A determination to keep my life simple and focused on myself and nothing else. I can tell it feels right. I don't feel nervous as I walk through the door.

'Hello stranger,' Carol shouts, from the reception desk.

'Hi Carol. How's things? Anything changed since I've been off?'

'The same old crap I'm afraid. Her lordship is micro-managing us. I've put a stone on by comfort eating. I shouldn't be saying this should I?' Carol sighs.

'Don't worry Carol. Just say it how it is.'

'Her Lordship is out for lunch at the moment; she should be back in about 15 minutes so go and chill in her office.'

Carol does look fuller around the face, but she looks better for it.

'I'll go and wait for her then,' I say, as I key in the code to open the door that leads to the stairs.

'Don't let her talk you into working all hours,' Carol shouts, as I walk through the door.

'Don't worry I won't,' I say, as I walk up the stairs.

I open the door to Jenny's office, and I'm surprised to see how untidy it is, there's paperwork everywhere. I've never really worked that closely with Jenny, so not sure if this is just the way she is, or she's struggling to keep organised. I pull the chair out from under the desk and sit down.

Blazon in a deep orange, blackness outlines the jungle trees on the eighth island as I look out from the seventh. Tranquil swamp waters, gently rippling like a peaceful lake. I desperately want to protect my life. I'm trying to keep my distance from Mike's negative energy. I need to be aware of the situations I place myself in and be selfish from now on, to ensure the safety of my inner-self and serenity.

Delicate pink and pale-whiteness of the orchids swaying in the gentle breeze; mesmerised as the orchid petals are captivated by the winds and pulled into the waters, I watch as they drift away and glide towards the eighth island. A cracking noise snaps me out of the trance I'm in. Look across towards the sheer cliff; the cliff-face is crumbling down, little by little, and the small rock-like pieces are tumbling into the lake which is why it is rippling. No panic, it feels quite comforting. Maybe it's because I no longer need my field. Maybe I'll no longer run into it, maybe I'll face up to things that are making me unhappy instead. Maybe I'll start to put *me* first. I don't know what 'maybe' is yet, but as I look up into the crystal-blue sky I feel calm and have peace of mind. I'm not ready to move from this island yet though. Lying down on the soft, green foliage as the waters gently ripple beside me, finding comfort in this peaceful atmosphere.

'Hi Lucy, how's things?' Jenny says, as she comes bounding into her office.

Long, straight, blonde hair that sits flat on her back. I watch as she throws her bag down on the floor and sits down on her chair to face me from across her desk. Do you know the saying, 'keep your enemies closer'? I get that feeling instantly. Not trusting anything about her and I don't think it's because of the way I am feeling, as I only get this vibe from her. She sits smiling at me like a smiling assassin. To my surprise I find it all amusing as I see the control freak for what she is.

'Okay Lucy, so how are you feeling? Do you feel ready to return to work next week?'

'Yes I do. I'm looking forward to coming back.'

'Okay, well there have been a few changes around here; a big, cost-cutting exercise. There's a rota now to cover the late shifts, so that overtime is not paid and you don't need to support the development of any written material, or leaflets.'

'Great, that's fine with me; not sure about late shifts though. What's all that about?'

'Well, everyone does one late shift once a fortnight.'

'Once I'm back to full time, working once a fortnight on a late shift sounds great. It's a lot better than working fifty-five hours a week and only getting paid for forty.'

She looks disappointed; the balance has shifted. She doesn't have control over me because the changes honestly don't bother me and by the look on her face she obviously presumed I got paid for the extra hours I did. I know; what a mug. But no more.

'So you never got paid for the extra hours then?'

'No I didn't,' I answer, surprised she didn't check that.

'I had to ask; it's my job. Okay, well come in on Tuesday, Wednesday and Friday and work five hours each day with no break.'

'Fine, I'll continue breaks when I get back full time. I always have my lunch at 1:30. I presume that's not changed?'

'That's fine, I've changed break and lunch times, but no one wants the 1:30 lunch; there's only you. So, lucky for you, that time is okay,' she says, with a smile.

'Lucky me, well if that's all, I'll get off now and see you Tuesday,' I say, as I stand up.

'See you Tuesday,' she says, as she looks down and starts writing on a pad of paper.

Smile to myself as I walk out of the room. Rick was right; I just didn't see it before. She's on her own power trip now, and it's a trip I don't want to be on.

I breeze out of the bank and escape onto the High Street. I promised Vicky I'd meet her for a coffee. I feel free. I'm starting to revert back to the way I felt pre-Mike. I walk towards the coffee shop and catch sight of Vicky sat at a table next to the window. Surprised to see Rick sat opposite her; that's a pleasant surprise.

'Do you want a coffee?' Rick asks, as I approach their table.

'Yes thanks, and it's nice to see you,' I say, as I give him a quick hug.

'You too; won't be a minute,' Rick says, as he heads to the service counter, rummaging for change in the pocket of his jeans.

'Hi Vicky,' I say, as I lean down and give her a hug before I pull the chair out and sit next to her.

'Well?' I continue and look over at Rick who's stood in a small queue at the service counter. I turn back to Vicky.

'Rick and I have been meeting each other quite a lot lately. We're trying to get to know each other as best friends. I still love him and don't want to make any hasty decisions and the thought of divorce knocks me sick,' Vicky says, as she looks over at Rick and smiles deeply at him.

'That's good. We'll have a proper girls' talk some time.'

'Well, what about you; how are you feeling?' Vicky asks and places her hand on my right shoulder for a quick touch of comfort.

'I'm fine. I'm back to work on Tuesday, so I'll be glad to get back to normal,' I sigh.

'And?' Vicky asks.

'Well, me and Mike have split up; I'm okay about it. One of us had to be brave and that person was me. I just need time on my own, to get myself together,' I say, as I stare at nothing.

'You'll be fine; you've got over the worst now. Rick and I never thought much of Mike but didn't like to say. But we will next time,' Vicky hastens to add.

'Melanie said the same; she's going to give any potential new boyfriend a once-over. Not that I'm interested in meeting anyone.'

'I know what you mean. I've been on a few nights out and I felt like a piece of meat; it certainly wasn't for me. I had a couple of clinches though but can't talk about that here. Come round to mine next Friday; Rick and I are still living apart and I've no intentions of living with him; not yet anyway.'

'Are you still living at the White House,' I laugh.

'Unfortunately, this recession has slowed the market down. We had one offer at fifty thousand below the asking price; cheeky aren't they,' Vicky says.

'Here you go,' Rick says, as he places the mugs of coffee on the table.

'Thanks.'

'Have you thought any more about moving to Liverpool?' Rick asks.

'Give her a chance Rick, she only starts back to work on Tuesday. Ignore him Lucy, he's always been pushy,' Vicky protests.

'It's fine Vicky. I have to be honest, Rick, I've had too much on. I feel that I should stay where I am, at least for now.

I want to get this sickness behind me, then I will definitely consider it; that's if the vacancy is still there then.'

'Of course, Lucy; there's always a job for you in Liverpool,' he says, as he lifts his large mug of coffee to take a sip.

'Thanks Rick, I appreciate it. I think you were right about Jenny; well, I know you were right. She's a right control freak.'

'Don't let her get to you. I think she's struggling. She's like a frightened child underneath the crap. She's always on the defensive in meetings and a complete control freak; paranoid in fact,' Rick says.

'Oh well, I'll watch my back and just do my job,' I say, as I sip my coffee.

'This looks cosy!'

We look up and are faced with Jenny.

'Hi Jenny,' I answer.

'This is nice; nice that you still care Rick.'

'Lucy is a good friend of Vicky's actually, and anyway what do you want? Can we help?'

'No, just commenting,' Jenny says, as she turns and walks away.

'I can't stand her. And there's nothing I can do because she's sleeping with some exec from head office' Rick says.

'You're joking!'

'No and I wouldn't mind but her current husband is a great person. She walks around acting as if she's flawless, yet she is full of lies. She lost touch with her first husband and son because of the lies. Constantly telling them she was working away when she was in Paris with some bloke she was having an affair with. Keep away from her Lucy, and don't get too involved with her personally, because she'll stop at nothing to protect her false, flawless image she has created. That's why she likes working with people who are new to the business or don't know any of her history. I wouldn't mind, but human beings can't possibly be perfect, we all make mistakes, so I've no idea why she is so vile and snide in hiding the truth.'

'Strong words Rick, don't let her get to you; she obviously isn't worth it. I'm determined she won't get to me,' I say, as I watch Jenny stood at the service counter. I can see that her hips have got more width to them, but as she once told me, no one tells you when you put on weight, so I won't say a word. And I can't help but think that Rick is really taking Jenny's attitude to heart; maybe he's trying to deflect from his own recent actions, or maybe he has my interests at heart and has seen an even more devious side of Jenny than we have. Oh well, bring on Tuesday.

* * *

Tuesday's here and I feel happy; happy to get ready and potter around the house before I leave for work. My mind is empty, so I have space to think and breathe.

'I can't believe you're going to that bitch's house on Friday,' Melanie snarls, as we're sat at our usual lunch-time bench at 08:30 in the morning as I can't have a lunchtime break today.

'Well, she asked me and, to be honest, I had quite a good time when I last saw her. She's a good hostess and serves great wine too. She had too much pressure with the two kids and being a wife. That's all changed, she's actually quite chilled and up for a laugh,' I say, as I look at Melanie. I can tell she's annoyed as she won't give me eye contact.

'Well, just don't ask me. I'll never speak to her again,' Melanie snaps.

'What's wrong with you today?'

'I'm just not in the mood to be honest. Paul's been made redundant; cutbacks hey?' Melanie storms.

'Really sorry Melanie; I didn't realise.'

'Well, I've not seen you for a while, have I? I'm just not much company these days,' she huffs, with her head bowed.

'Come round to mine if you need to escape from it all; you know where I am,' I say, as I watch her trapping herself emotionally with the negative thinking.

Melanie's negative aura is trying to pull me in, but I now listen to other people's problems without getting involved. I try to keep my nose out these days, though it's hard as I genuinely care.

Rising waters; rising up to my knees; no longer able to sit down; look across to the cliff-face. It is disappearing by the day; the crumbling pieces are larger and causing tidal ripples in the waters surrounding this island. The orange sun is peering behind broken cloud and shining down onto the rippled water, which looks like broken glass against this light. The eighth island is blazon in blackness against orange landscape within the surrounding air. I can see a faint outline of mountains in the distance; it must be the mainland of my journey.

Paddling towards the edge of the seventh island, look back towards the centre. Water, swishing against my knees; freezing-cold, penetrating through to my bone; still hesitant and unable to move forward. Pausing and checking in on myself each day to make sure the focus is still on me. Life seems simple as I am learning to detach myself from negative energy and no longer go on the defensive. I can see things for what they truly are and I can see people for who they are.

* * *

'So you will all have access to the appointment diary and whenever a customer comes to our branch, I expect you to do a quick check on their accounts to see if they need any extra borrowing,' Jenny announces, at our Tuesday morning meeting.

We're crammed into her office space; files piled on top of each other. She's making more work for herself; what happened to our paperless office? There are small, plastic crates crammed into one corner of the room; looks like it's from her previous branch, as I can see a hole-punch and a broken-glass picture frame. She obviously hasn't unpacked properly. And she obviously treats her office as her home; probably doesn't have the fabulous life outside of work. When I think back she never really talked about her fabulous life and I kind of feel sorry for her ... for a fleeting second that is.

'But some customers are in a rush; they just want to pay money in. They don't always have time to hang around and the queue can get too big if we don't hurry it up,' I respond.

'Is that negativity I can hear? You will follow this or go through the disciplinary process, and for those who don't hit the stringent targets, you'll be going down the capability process,' Jenny says, as she looks at me sternly, opens a file and rummages through the pages. Black mark for me I suppose.

Plunge into the waters; tepid feeling as I submerge ... clear waters. Clarity and warmth in my heart as I slowly wade amongst the floating orchid petals. Easiness as I use my arms to keep balanced within shadowed waters as I near the island. Freedom in my step as I prevent myself from becoming weighed down; not reacting to Jenny's snarly attitude. I see it for what it is, and it's hers not mine; she can keep it.

'No, it's just a fact. We need to look at how this can logically work,' I answer.

'Just do it. I expect you to try and make appointments and I've adjusted the system so you can enter your name against the appointment date and time. I'll be monitoring how many appointments each of you make. We need to increase the sales in this branch,' Jenny announces, quite defensively.

'I don't think doing it whilst the customer just wants to pay money in is the right thing to do,' Carol adds.

'Don't you?' Jenny says and doesn't say anything else.

'Okay. Well, you know what needs to be done. I'll review it this week and let you know how each of you do next week; name and shame if you don't do well,' Jenny laughs.

'I can't be doing with this; whatever happened to the simple days,' Mary sighs, as she signs into her workstation.

'I'll go and get our coffees,' Carol shouts, as I catch a glimpse of her flying out of the door and onto the High Street.

Pull myself out of the water and onto the eighth island. Stand back and look on in awe. Sheer green of the foliage tumbling down from its branches in layers, dullness of the low-level shrubbery shaded amongst the jungle trees. I'm captivated by the sunlight, cascading over high-level branches and foliage, changing the colour of the leaves from green to yellow. A stream of shallow, clear water gently meanders through the centre of the island, reflecting the jungle upon the calm waters. There are large, grey-coloured stepping stones and small embankments of gravelled shale which will allow me to cross from one side of this island to the other.

'There you go Lucy,' Carol says, with a smile as she hands me a coffee.

'Thanks Carol'.

* * *

'She won't come,' I say to Vicky.

Vicky and I are sat in her living-room, having a few glasses of wine. She desperately wants Melanie to come, but Melanie has already warned me she never would.

'I'll ring her, but I doubt she'll come over,' I say, as I rummage in my handbag for my mobile phone.

'I'll go and get another bottle of wine,' Vicky says, as she stands up and walks out of the room.

'I don't know how you can drink red wine so fast; I've not even finished my first glass and you'll be on your third,' I shout, as I dial Melanie's phone number on my mobile.

'Melanie, it's Lucy. I know you said not to ask, but I'm at Vicky's house and she really wants you to come round,' I whisper.

Vicky comes bounding into the room with another bottle of red wine and grabs the phone out of my hand.

'Melanie, it's Vicky, I'm really, really sorry for being a spoilt bitch in the past; that honestly wasn't me. It was the pregnancy hormones and desperate housewife inside of me,' she laughs. 'Great, see you soon,' she shouts, and throws the phone at me ... literally.

'She's coming; she'll be here in five minutes, and Paul's dropping her off.'

I don't answer as a feeling of dread consumes me. Vicky seems a bit weird tonight, a bitch on a mission. She looks uneasy as she sits on the settee pouring herself another glass of wine. In no mood for any dramas, all I can do is sit back and see what happens.

Feelings of uneasiness overwhelm me as the doorbell rings. Knowing it's Melanie and her feelings towards Vicky are not exactly positive ... nowhere near. Vicky leaps up off the settee and speed-walks out of the room.

'Take a seat,' Vicky says, as she leads Melanie into the room.

Melanie has the word project written all over her face; serious but amused. She sits next to me as Vicky leaves the room to get her a glass.

'This should be interesting,' Melanie says, with a smile.

'What do you mean?' I ask.

'That big arsehole told Vicky about Project Sandwich,' Melanie announces.

'What are you on about,' I ask, as I sit bolt upright and feel freshly sober.

'Andy went out with Vicky last week, she got him drunk, and he told her that we found them in that bloody sandwich van. That's why I jumped at the chance to come round. I only found out tonight when I saw Andy; he was red-faced when he told me but glad he had the guts to let me know. I thought about you being here and I was going to text but knew it was too late as you'd already be here. But don't worry, I'm here for you,' Melanie says, as she gives me one of her reassuring but sarcastic rubs on my shoulder.

I look at her and sip my wine; she absolutely loves this. She's bracing herself for the impact. Looking perversely happy, in her element, like a pig in mud, like a duck in water, like a kid in a sweet shop; you get my drift. All I can do is smile to myself. Best to get it all out in the open I suppose.

I gasp to myself as I remember back to when I was here last, comforting Vicky and not letting on that I knew. This will certainly test my new way of thinking.

'Are you making that glass?' Melanie shouts.

'Sorry, I had to nip to the loo. Coming now,' Vicky shouts.

'Hope you washed your hands,' Melanie shouts, and winks at me. 'I know her husband doesn't,' she whispers to me.

I can't believe I'm back here; like being back on the floor behind the sandwich van. I can't control Vicky or Melanie so I'd best just try and remain positive.

'More wine Lucy?' Vicky asks.

'No, thanks,' I say and sip my wine so she can't force a top-up.

'Right to the top for me Vicky,' Melanie says.

'I don't suppose you've got a sandwich, or anything have you Vicky? I missed out on chippy tea,' Melanie asks.

I start coughing and nearly choke on my wine.

'God Lucy, have you been eating spicy sausage and meatballs for your tea, you know they give you bad heart burn,' Melanie asks, as she vigorously pats my back and smirks at me.

'I can't eat spicy food either,' Vicky says, as she sits down.

'I can eat and drink anything; I'm starving,' Melanie announces.

'Sorry Melanie, I've got a leaflet for pizza delivery; let's order something, my treat, I'll get the leaflet,' Vicky says, as she stands up and walks out of the room.

'I can't take it,' I laugh, and put my wine glass down on the table before I spill any. 'Come on Melanie, not tonight, it's exhausting,' I plead.

Melanie doesn't answer; she sips her wine and looks very pleased with herself. She's very comfortable in these situations, which makes me feel better, but also freaks me out a bit.

As I look around the room, the place doesn't seem as grand as it did the first time I was here. All of the pictures have been taken down and it looks like some furniture has been moved.

'Have you moved things around in here or something?' I ask Vicky, as she walks back in the room and hands Melanie the pizza leaflet.

'I've boxed a lot of stuff up. Did I tell you about that offer we had which was £50k under budget? Well they put in a better offer. It's still £20k under, but I'm still left with £80k to go towards my next house. I put in an offer for another house and they accepted £8k less than what they were asking, so looks like it's all falling into place,' Vicky replies.

I can see Melanie's starting to seethe, but it's not as if Vicky is being hard-faced as she has been in the past. It's probably because of Melanie's husband's situation. I do feel like a rose between two thorns here and there's nothing I can do.

'Oh, before I forget Melanie, my brother Mark wanted me to give you his number. He wants your Paul to ring him; there might be a job for him at Mark's place. Mark's opening a second branch and said your Paul would be ideal to manage it,' Vicky says, with a smile.

'How does Mark know Paul?' Melanie asks, with a calmer attitude.

'Paul did a few jobs for Mark and he was really impressed; said he's a grafter and good with people. He needs someone he can trust,' Vicky answers. 'Let Paul know now.

Mark was hoping to catch up with him tomorrow or Sunday,' Vicky continues.

'I think I'll ring him now; can I ring from your kitchen,' Melanie asks.

'Sure,' Vicky says.

Melanie gets up and skulks out of the room with her tail between her legs.

'Are you surprised?' Vicky asks me.

'I am, considering you two never get on.'

'Well, I like Paul; that's why I asked how his job was when I last saw her, as Mark had heard that there may be redundancies. He really wants Paul to work for him. I couldn't believe it when Melanie responded the way she did. Well, that was until I had an interesting night out with Andy,' Vicky says, and examines me for a reaction.

'Well, how could we possibly tell you,' I say, as the heat rises in my face with uncomfortable embarrassment.

'I admire the pair of you for being respectful over it; well, except for the attitude that is, but then who could blame Melanie? I was a bitch and I can admit that now. I just didn't realise at the time. But to hide the fact you knew about Rick's deceit … we're meant to be *friends*. I was fuming when Andy told me; it took me days to calm down. My mum made me see sense, made me see things from your point of view. I know it must have been awkward working with Rick, but please you must always be open with me; I will be with you,' Vicky says, and sips her wine. I can't answer her, as there is no reasonable answer. Unsure if that's because of my guilt and embarrassment; knowing she deserved better from us.

'Paul's going to ring Mark now,' Melanie announces, as she walks into the room.

'Great, well, no more secrets or bitchiness,' Vicky shouts, and lifts her glass. We clink our glasses. Melanie looks a little uncertain.

'Well, what pizza do you want?' Vicky asks.

'I'll have a look now,' Melanie says, and reads through the leaflet.

'Just don't turn into a bitch when Paul is managing the new branch,' Vicky laughs.

'As if,' Melanie laughs back.

Sitting up and taking in the beauty of the eighth island, warmth in the air as the sun glares heat and light.

* * *

I smile to myself as I wake up in bed; the events of the night before make me laugh. Feeling settled and at peace as I step out of bed, put on my dressing gown and walk downstairs. The dog clambers out of the house when I open the back door, put on the kettle and walk into the living room. It's so nice to have actual physical peace as well as peace of mind. Settling down on the settee with a cup of tea.

Sudden, loud, constant knocking on the door. I can't be bothered answering. But it's clear the knocking isn't going to stop, so I begrudgingly get up to answer.

'Hello Mike,' I say, as I open the door to his stony, miserable face. He instantly marches into the house.

'I got you the paper,' he says, as he looks around the house and then sits in what was his chair. 'What are you up to today?' he asks.

'I'm just chilling.'

'Not today. I need some company today,' he says, as he crouches on the floor next to where I'm sitting.

'I've got plans; I was looking forward to having a day to myself,' I answer.

'Not today you're not. I'm lonely, I can't cope in that flat any longer,' he announces.

'Well get a hobby; go and see your friends or family.'

'I'm lonely,' he announces, as he starts to prod and torment me.

'You can't do this,' I say.

'I can. I don't want you to find anyone else,' he says.

'I won't; not that it has anything to do with you. I don't want anyone else. I've got to go shopping anyway,' I announce, and get up.

'I'll come with you; I need some bits,' he says, as he follows me into the kitchen and asks for a hug.

This is the first time he's been round. I've managed to keep away from him but I suppose it was only a matter of time. Now what am I meant to do?

Chapter 9

To succeed in life, you need two things; ignorance and confidence. Mark Twain

Stood amongst green foliage on the eighth island, feel paralysed and breathless as I look down-stream; clinging onto the jungle tree. I want to cross the stream to explore, but all I can do is hug the trunk as I contemplate moving forward with my life, daring to move out of my comfort zone with a confidence that has been lost somewhere. I know I'll sink if I push myself too far.

A flash of red catches my eye as it flies past and lands on a branch over the other side of the stream. A pale, naked, gangly branch, rope-like in its appearance as it sways slightly when the redness touches it. More redness flies, squawking in its flight, perching on the branch. An urge to move forward to take a closer look as more redness flies with such speed and elegance; crouching down, unsure if I should move.

Fingertips scraping against the trunk of the tree as I step towards the stream. A feeling of departure as I let go. Dare to move away from the comfort and feel of the secluded security. A false security hidden from reality.

Flight of freedom ... freedom in my heart and soul, exhilarated laughter, uncontrollable. No care or concern in this moment; laughing with friends, about nothing in particular, noticing everything around me. Pale-blue and orange sky. Beaten pathways, ancient architecture hidden amongst the new, a free heart and mind as we enter the coffee shop. Streaming tears, hanging on to each other, not wanting to let go of this moment.

'I've got something to tell the two of you,' Vicky says, as we sit down to eat lunch. 'Rick and I are renewing our wedding vows,' she gasps, with bright, sparkly eyes.

'Congratulations,' I say, with a smile.

'I'm not saying anything,' Melanie answers, and then sips coffee.

'Thanks for not being bitchy,' Vicky says to Melanie.

'We've been going for counselling for three months; going as a couple and separately. I had to figure out if I could forgive Rick and if I still loved him, and I do,' Vicky sighs.

'That's great, so have you had sex with him yet?'

'Trust you Melanie!' Vicky storms.

'Well?' Melanie asks.

'Yes, yes we have, but I'm back on the pill. No more kids for me and don't look at me like that Melanie. I know you must think I'm mad, but Rick was tested for everything and we use condoms. And I know he betrayed me, but I betrayed him too with my neglect and ignorance towards our marriage; I completely ignored our wedding vows. I was more interested in the big, white house and keeping that clean and tidy,' Vicky announces.

'Do you know what? It's important to work at it, if you truly believe you're with the one,' Melanie says.

'I'm filling up,' Vicky says, as she gazes sarcastically at Melanie.

'Well, it's true. I truly love Paul and we went to counselling for a while. It was the best thing we ever did. Just because he wasn't unfaithful doesn't mean he didn't do anything else to hurt me. But come to think of it, it was me who hurt him with my jealousy and insecurity,' Melanie says.

'Will you help me find a dress?' Vicky asks.

'As long as the kids aren't with us; kids and shopping don't mix,' Melanie urges.

'They won't be with us and do you know what? I can't wait. I've never felt happier and I promise it won't be back to Victoria,' Vicky laughs.

'Rick's going to move into the new house with me and we'll stay there. We want fun; don't want to be up to our eyeballs again,' Vicky gushes.

'And before you ask about Andy, we'll never speak to him again. How can we? I still think he took advantage of Rick when Rick had a few too many to drink and was feeling vulnerable, but Rick won't have it; he's taking responsibility for it all. Andy and I just ignore each other now. Rick doesn't see him since he changed jobs, and things are alright really. I know you must wonder how I can get intimate with Rick, but it happens all the time these days; sometimes the gender of a person doesn't come into it when someone strays. I can't blame Rick for everything, the two of us abandoned our relationship, I realise that now. I heard Andy's moving down south with some new fella he's met. A fresh start all round. We just need to get you paired up Lucy,' Vicky continues.

'Don't even think of that. I've no intention of pairing with anyone. I don't mind meeting new friends, but nothing else,' I say.

'Friends with benefits,' Melanie winks.

'No chance. Just friends and I'm being serious.'

Cautiously step onto the large, grey stone that's protruding from the stream of water. Take care with each step forward onto the next stone. Looking down into the clear, shallow stream, appreciate the pureness and clarity as I see my reflection in the still water. Recognising myself again, feeling stronger and more able, but still lacking confidence.

Squawking. Tremendous sound filters through the air. Step onto the embankment on the other side of the island. Look up into the clear-blue sky, broken by a flash of redness. Bold red and blue, gliding through the air above my eye-line, wings stretched out, glorified in colour. Wings blazoned in red, merging into a lightness of green, true blueness and tipped in a deep blue, pure beyond words. Look on in awe, dozens of macaws, perched on naked branches. A blanket of macaws cling onto a crumbling, clay wall; a wall hiding behind the vast amount of foliage and branches. Colour, light and sound being brought back to life before my very eyes and assailing my ears. Echoes of sound, alarming, juddering through my entire body as I approach the wall. Fingertips against the grainy feel; coldness, pure, refined grit that crumbles when touched. Feel the wall as I glide the palm of my left hand; sharpness against my skin. Sudden movement underfoot, vibrations, instant flight as the macaws escape in their flock, leaping from the wall and the safety of the branches. Searing sound, hypnotic exit as they pierce the sky and out of sight.

'Here she is,' Carol shouts, as I rush through the door to work.

'I'm not late, I've got a few minutes.'

'We're not worried about that. Jenny's not here anymore,' Carol says.

'I'll go and put my bag in the locker; you can update me when I get back down,' I shout, as I input the security number and open the door that leads to the stairs.

I rush back down the stairs to log into my workstation, hoping there's no big queue so Carol can update me on the amazing news.

'Okay come on,' I shout, as I log in.

'I'll come to you. You'll see it on email anyway, but I can tell you the story before you open your mailbox,' Carol says.

'Not if you carry on as you are without actually telling me. Come on,' I demand, impatiently.

'There's an email from Jenny saying she's going back to her previous branch. Pam is coming here in her place. She said her stay here was only temporary until Pam could increase her hours back to full time. Pam's only been able to do that now since returning from maternity leave,' Carol announces.

'Okay,' I say.

'She also thanked us for welcoming her; can you believe that?' Carol says.

'Well, maybe she can be challenged more there. I know she has a great relationship with the girls in that branch. Not sure what happened when she came here.'

I open my mailbox to read the email for myself; no feelings when I read it and no urge to reply. I delete the email and get on with my work.

'Jenny's handing over to Pam today so she'll be with us tomorrow,' Carol shouts.

'Great,' I say, sarcastically.

* * *

'Hi everybody,' Pam says, as she comes bounding into the office.

'Hi Pam,' Carol says, 'we weren't expecting you till tomorrow.'

'Well, Jenny doesn't need a hand-over and I wanted to come over ASAP to get to know you all,' Pam says, with a smile. A friendly, inviting smile and I know it's genuine somehow. She has cropped, dark-brown hair with a tinge of grey; long, narrow face with smooth, defined cheekbones. She's wearing a grey, tailored suit, shiny-black stilettos, and wheeling a small laptop case. I don't sense any type of threat at all.

'I'll show you round and introduce you to everyone,' Carol offers.

'Thanks Carol,' Pam says, and follows her as they walk through the door that leads to the stairs.

'She seems nice,' Mary says.

'Yes she does. Well, here's hoping,' I say, as the first customer stands at my workstation.

* * *

'Your turn to go up,' Carol shouts, as she walks out of the door from the stairway.

'Oh, okay. What for?'

'Pam's settled into the office already. We had a chat and now she wants to chat with everyone. You're next,' Carol announces.

Lock my workstation and make my way upstairs to meet Pam.

'Hi Lucy, sit down,' she says, as I open the door and walk into the room. Sitting opposite, I glance around, shocked to see all of Jenny's stuff has gone.

'Okay Lucy, I've been looking at your file since I found out I was going to be working here last week, and I think we need a good chat,' Pam smiles.

'Okay, what about?' I ask.

'I spoke to Rick about you, and he agrees that you need to push yourself a little bit more; you're more than capable,' Pam says. 'You won that competition didn't you. Your product has been developed now, so we need you to work on it for a week before it gets mass-produced,' Pam says.

'Honestly?' I ask.

'Of course, Lucy, why wouldn't I be honest? Even Jenny said she couldn't get through to you about development and she said if anything you've taken a big leap backwards. We need to get your fire back,' Pam says, with a smile. 'I want you to work in Manchester for a week, review the material now that it has been developed. You need to spend three weeks moving around our branches to roll it out,' Pam continues.

'I'd love to,' I say.

'Okay then, you'll work in Manchester from Monday for a week. I'll have a plan after that and let you know where you'll be working. I probably shouldn't say this, but you also need to watch your back. There are a lot of people who are out for themselves,' Pam sighs. 'That's all for today. You need to get moving Lucy; you did really well to win the competition, embrace it.'

Look towards the clay wall which is now laid bare. It's a fragile exposure of cracks and deformities; no longer hidden but still holding in-depth strength, posture and purpose. Tranquil air surrounds the mass of jungle trees and foliage; walking alongside the stream to get to the other side of this island. Coldness in the shade; yearning for the warmth of the sun as it scorches the trees overhead. Feel the leathery, green leaves and cup the thin, gangly trunks of the jungle trees with my hands; using them as a crutch as I journey forward. A gentle flowing stream in this calm environment; have peace of mind, feel safe, but forcing myself to stride forward and finish my journey. No longer want to stay here and hide away, even in all its beauty and entirety. Understanding that ignorance, denial and self-pity are unhealthy but human feelings I had to dissect. Want to manage myself better, but knowing progress not perfection is where I am. Stream's sudden end; shaded, moss-covered stones forged together in a pile. Narrow rushes of white water running downwards, forcing entry into the stream. Tangled jungle foliage, tumbling ivy, knotted orchids, green fern, clumsily grown together. Struggle to walk through the entanglement, standing on entwined branches, bending and breaking them underfoot; forcing my way through to break free to the other side of this island. Damp, darkened, decayed feel. Slimy feel to the touch as moss thrives in this environment. Growing light ahead as daylight seeps through the tangled branches. Seeing a way forward I find the energy to force myself through. Dragging, using the bulky branches to pull myself to an opening in the foliage.

* * *

I'm relieved to see that the building in Manchester isn't like the one in my dream. It's certainly not an expensive, glamorous place; it looks lifeless, grey and dank from the outside. The reception area is quite small; the receptionist is wearing a uniform, but it's a boring navy-blue which is a relief. Everything seems normal.

Suffocating inside, I step into the lift; it must be the smallest lift I've ever stood in, so it's quite a relief when it reaches the second floor, and the doors open. Narrow, dingy corridors, old decor and navy-blue carpeting; musty smell, dust particles glisten against the sun as it seeps through the small, high-level windows. Newer buildings are open plan and allow more light; they breathe life.

The door to the office is ajar so I step inside. 'Hello,' I say, as I see a woman sat at a desk looking out of the window.

She turns around to look at me. 'Hello, you must be Lucy. I'll be showing you around, letting you know where the fire exits are etcetera, and more importantly where the break-out areas are, though we tend to go out for lunch. Follow me, I'll show you round. My name's Jane by the way.'

I am actually here, living in this very moment, not living in yesterday or thinking about tomorrow; no, just today, now. I follow Jane as she leads me down the narrow corridor, along a maze of corridors. Jane has cropped, bleach-blonde hair and sparkly-blue eyes that glisten when she speaks. Far too much energy and vibrancy to be stuck in this maze, like a hamster on a wheel.

'Come on, we're having a coffee before I show you were you're going to be working,' Jane says, with a smile as we walk into the break-out area. An enclosed room with striking, white floor and walls. The lack of colour beams out against the metal-framed windows; dried rain dirties the view onto the grey-coloured city. Sun breaks out from behind grey cloud, shining down onto the city street below; rain pouring towards multi-coloured umbrellas and rushing feet.

'How do you like your coffee?' Jane asks.

'Black for me,' I answer, and look around.

Sit down at a small, square table that seats four. Watch Jane as she excitedly talks to a male employee in the queue. Operatic in her pose and expression, she probably doesn't even see it herself, otherwise she wouldn't be here. He's amused, all six foot of him, pure-black hair, expensive tailoring, and chocolate-brown eyes.

'Here you go,' Jane says, as she places our mugs of coffee on the table and sits down. 'So Lucy, tell me a bit about yourself,' she asks.

Pause before I answer, purposely wanting to be as boring as possible, knowing she will soon get fed up. 'I've worked at the bank for years now and I'm really looking forward to a change,' I say, with a blank expression, desperately determined not to give anything away.

'Okay, well we can head there now if you want,' Jane grunts.

'Okay, that'd be great,' I say, as I stand up.

Feel instantly relieved as she leads me into a large, open-plan room. Plenty of daylight beaming through the large, metal-framed windows that run across the entire back wall. Blinds prevent the sun from searing in.

'You'll be working here,' Jane says, as she stops at a desk. Restlessness from Jane as she fidgets impatiently, unable to stand still, be at peace with herself. Desperately wanting to move away from my calm energy and flitter back out to wander the corridors of gossip and tales.

'I've just got to meet someone, so I'll catch up with you in a bit,' she says, as she turns to rush off out of the room.

'So much for fire exits,' I think to myself.

Trapped, entangled, suffocating, fight with myself, encased within the jungle foliage. This time with realisation and understanding of my feelings; identifying with myself. I can see my reaction, no longer able to act or be a robot. Emotions and feelings at my grasp, no longer introvert, finally admitting that I am a human being who won't cope with everything.

No longer prepared to hold onto any worry I send an email to Pam telling her that I don't want to go around the branches to present the material. She'll probably think I'm mad as someone else will take the glory for my work, but I can't worry about that now.

Relief as I step out of the foliage, and immediately feel the warm air. Lightened skies and sandy floor on this side of the island; dirty, a mix of sand and soil, rather than pure sand, as if the atmosphere is trying to change. Look out across to the ninth island. Still, blue waters separate from where I'm stood. Overpowering jungle-foliage and trees, a confused mix within the atmosphere, a vague transition from this world, but not enough clarity to understand or see it clearly, familiar sounds fade into the distance, but can't quite hear. A gentle nudge, a shake to awaken me, but confusion prevents me from feeling or seeing the trueness.

* * *

'It's good to see that Andy isn't chief bridesmaid,' Melanie sniggers, as we're stood near the front of the church, waiting for Vicky to walk down the aisle.

'Do you think we're sat on the right side?' I ask, looking over at Rick's side of the seats.

'Well, I think we'll leave Rick to worry about that one, let's hope he's on the right side,' Melanie laughs.

'Will you stop it,' I laugh. 'It could be worse; we could have agreed to be bridesmaids,' I add.

'Don't. Can you imagine that? What was she thinking, asking us and why renew vows in a church? Why not do it quietly, on their own, abroad somewhere?' Melanie asks.

'She's here now,' I say, as we all stand up; gentle music playing.

Beautiful Vicky and her o.t.t. dress make their way down the aisle. She's definitely making a statement; she got her man.

Distracted by a consuming energy, I look over at Rick; he's glaring at me. He quickly turns to watch Vicky walk down the aisle. He'd best not give me a hard time about not wanting to deliver the insurance material.

Grainy sand particles run through my fingers as I feel the sandy floor with both hands. I'm happy to sit confused, but more aware. I don't want to waste time looking back, but I feel a desire to be aware of past mistakes and decisions without regret. Look towards the ninth island in all its glory with pure-white sands, as turquoise waters lap towards it and then pull back in tidal rhythm.

Vibrating handbag against my thigh betraying a buzzing mobile phone inside my bag; no doubt receiving abusive texts from Mike, because he knows I'm at the wedding and I will be staying for the evening entertainment. I've been trying to keep out of his way. I don't want to see him again.

'Even I feel like filling up,' Melanie says, as she wipes her face with a tissue.

'It was lovely wasn't it,' I say, knowing I didn't even see any of the wedding service, too preoccupied.

* * *

'It's only ten o'clock Lucy; stop being so miserable,' Melanie seethes, in a drunken stupor.

'I'm not miserable; I just need to get going. You'll have a great time; you won't even notice I'm not here.' I walk away with a cloud of dust behind me as I take it all in my stride.

Peace in my mind as I drive home. No worry or concern as I drive the car into my driveway. Suddenly filled with horror; Mike is kneeling down next to my front door. I don't want him here or in my house, so I don't get out of the car. Try to remain calm; need to have my wits about me. Wind the window down a little but keep the car engine running and the doors locked. He stands up and walks towards me.

'What are you doing here, it's late?' I ask.

'I was just passing so I wanted to say hello.'

'Well, I'm up early in the morning so I can't talk to you.'

'Can you give me lift home then? Go on, it won't take you long and you'll get rid of me quicker.'

'Get in then,' I say, as I unlock the doors.

A familiar stench of alcohol consumes the car as he sits in the passenger seat. A stench I'd forgotten about. Consumed with familiar feelings I've not felt for a while, fear, dread, pain. A sickness I've not stomached since he left. Drunken words leave his mouth, but I can't hear what he is saying. Panic-stricken, I can't even look at him; it's completely haunting me and my racing brain is trying to think of a way out.

'You can get out the car now,' I say, as I bring the car to a sudden stop near to where he lives.

'Who the fuck do you think you are, to tell me to get out now?' he rages.

'Just get out, I can't stand you,' I say, without looking at him. I just focus on the steering wheel as he gleefully laughs in complete enjoyment. He's got me where he wants me.

Blackness, sheer blackness, stranded with the pure, whirling strength of the wind, driving spears as cold as ice, and as hard as steel through my heart. Dejected, unable to move as freezing-cold waters wash over me. Slumped on the floor of the eighth island, head in hands, unable to think clearly or see how I can move from here. I wish I had an ejector seat; I'd immediately eject him out of my car and out of my life. I can't stand it, sat here, not even listening to him. I'm not listening to the words, just completely haunted by the sound. Try my best to blank Mike out of my hearing, out of my sight, as I purposely don't look at him. I feel physically sick and completely traumatised. Realise that all I'm feeling is inward again; outwardly I look calm and I'm not reacting to him. He can't see that he *is* affecting me and I sense he is now getting bored, as his manipulation as much as he can see, is not working. Continue to blank him out and feel relief when he finally gets out of the car. His slam of the door is all I need to speed away, get out of there and away from him as quickly as possible.

Racing heart and mind; real pain in my stomach and down my legs. Turn off the engine as I park on my driveway. I'm desperate to get back into the safety of my home as I turn the key and open the door. The feeling is a complete slap in the face and another wake up call. Realisation that I can't rely on the jungle to escape; I have to set healthy boundaries in my life and just be with people I can be myself with. Traumatised as I stumble into the freezing waters to journey to the ninth island, determined that I never want to feel like this again. Relieved I no longer live in chaos and self-respect growing in the knowledge I never will again. Full moon lighting a pathway against the freezing waters, reflection of whiteness against the blackness of the night. Absolute determination in every step as I wade forward, take care with every move; to move on with my life.

Chapter 10

I'm enjoying life, feeling alive, living in the day and working hard. My fitness plan is back on track, though these bingo wings are more of a challenge than I thought, but I watched a programme on TV and an expert said we store fat in the top of our arms. It'll be a targeted distraction and a major focus. I'm having fun too; been out with friends to watch comedians on tour, vintage clothes shows and fairs, shopping and lunching in cities and the odd glass of red wine when I'm out and about.

'No, I won't change my mind,' I say, as I end the call on my mobile.

Rick is trying to talk me into travelling around the different branches to present and explain the product. He said he's drawn up a plan with Pam, so that one of them are with me; they want to assess me anyway. He said he knows that once I get over this hurdle, I'll get my confidence back. Maybe they're right.

Rick's invited me to their house on Friday for a dinner party. Melanie and Paul are going, along with Vicky's brother Mark and his wife. Should be a good night then.

* * *

I can't help but smile as I pull on my knitted hat and wrap the knitted scarf around my neck; a smile that represents freedom of choice. Laugh to myself as I look down at my new, fitted, electric-blue dress, as blue as my eyes. Check my make-up in the mirror that's fixed to the wall in the hallway. The nights are drawing in and cold now; I declined Melanie's offer of a lift as there's something magical about being wrapped up and going for a brisk walk on a crisp, winter evening. I need to acclimatise myself, ready for the true winter freeze. Christmas is looming; I love the run up to it and the fact I'm on my own hasn't changed that feeling. Button up my baby-pink, woollen, winter coat, put on my leather gloves and pick up the carrier bag containing a couple of bottles of red wine.

Torched moonlight lightens the clear, still sky, radiating light like a lighthouse, across the atmosphere and enlightening the waters which look as still and as hard as a clean blackboard. Look back towards the near-invisible eighth island as it distances itself. Sharpened wind forges through me and towards the centre of this island. Stood at the water's edge with a feeling of strength and hope, value and love for myself.

Enveloped by the strength of the wind, as I stumble upon the deep, sandy floor, contemplating my journey.

Freezing air enraptures my face, a spring in each step, absolute freedom as I walk to Vicky's house. Dazzling headlights strain my eyes as traffic whizzes past, splattering wetness as tyres drone against the dampened roads. Squelchy and slippery underfoot, orange and brown leaves fused onto the pathways. A feeling of self-protection against the hazardous conditions. Look ahead, looking forward to seeing Rick and Vicky's new, more-manageable home. Hope it's filled with love and laughter rather than an empty soul of a place.

Blackness; true-black outline of the jungle trees and foliage against the navy-blue of the darkened, night sky. A little lost and unable to see where I'm truly going. Unafraid of this place though; feel safe as I look towards the dark outline of a single mountain in the distance. The only light is from the illuminating moonlight, no stars or cloud to be seen, just a blanket of blue. Searing cold, sharpness in my feet, as I trudge in the deep coldness of the sand; ice-cold feel as I journey forwards. Certain the sand won't be as deep towards the centre of the island; the ninth, and I really hope this journey ends soon. Reach for the foliage as I step within the entanglement of the branches, feel safe as they encase me. No longer able to see the mountain in the distance, know I have to just deal with the *here and now*.

Pull down the latch on the small, black, metal gate, step onto the narrow pathway that leads to Vicky's front door. Large, semi-detached house, immaculately trimmed hedges to the right of the walkway. A polished-black, painted doorway, surrounded by original, stained-glass window. There'll always be a bit of Victoria in here somewhere. Original, open porch, dull red and yellow, square tiles on the floor just outside of the front door. Cream, roll-down blinds, tightly closed on the living-room bay window. Gloved finger pressed against the bell.

'Hi Lucy; can't believe you've walked,' Vicky says, as she opens the door.

'I wanted to build up an appetite,' I say, as I step into the house. Don't want to admit I'm freezing to the bone.

'Give us a hug; you look lovely and snug. I love the coat,' Vicky says, as she wraps her arms around me.

'It's cold out,' I say, as I hug her. We pull away from each other with a smile and I start unbuttoning my coat.

An unrecognisable, male figure distracts me as I look into the front room; a man I definitely haven't set my eyes on and all I can think of is 'hat hair', and panic.

'I'll just nip to the loo and then you can introduce me to everyone. Here I bought a couple of bottles of red wine,' I say, as I give her the bag that contains the two bottles of wine.

'Sure; the bathroom is upstairs or there's the downstairs' toilet by the front door,' Vicky says, with a smile.

'I'll go upstairs,' I say, as I hand Vicky my coat, hat and scarf.

I place my gloves in my bag and walk up the stairs to the bathroom. A very spacious room with a separate shower cubicle and bath, and thankfully there's a full-length mirror. I turn my head upside down to buff-up my flat, hat hair. I touch-up my lipstick and look at myself in the mirror.

'Stop being a stupid cow,' I say to myself. I'm not here to be paired up anyway. He may have his wife with him. I need to stop worrying, chill out; I am allowed to have male friends. I smile as I check myself out. My eyes are definitely sparkling tonight against this electric-blue dress. Honey-blonde, bobbed hair has bounced back to life. Life is what I see and feel as I take a closer look at myself, spirit behind my eyes, burning fire of a spirit inside of me. An energy I'm struggling to contain, on the verge of bursting. Feel confident as I open the bathroom door and walk downstairs. Smile broadly at Vicky as she stands at the bottom with a large glass of red wine in her hand. Awareness that I have to protect this brief moment of confidence.

'Thanks Vicky,' I say, as I take the glass of wine out of her hand.

Vicky places her hand on my shoulder and gently leads me into the living room. Melanie and Paul are sat on the settee. Melanie springs up to give me a hug.

'You look great,' Melanie says, as she practically hugs the life out of me.

'Thanks Melanie. Hi Paul.'

'Hi Lucy, nice to see you,' he says, with a smile as he relaxes on the settee. I can see and feel his happiness as he glances up towards Melanie.

'This is my brother Mark and his wife Susan,' Vicky says.

'Nice to meet you both,' I say, as I shake their hands. Mark oozes confidence, verging on being cocky. A confidence I recognise from Vicky before her troubles started with Rick. He has dark-brown hair, slightly greying at the sides. Moisturised, smooth, clean-shaven skin, large, brown eyes and full lips. I can't help but think he looks a little like Rick. Susan on the other hand is stick-thin, immaculately dressed in a fitted, black dress to the knee. Sheer-black, shoulder-length hair that slightly drains her complexion, but her red lipstick and long eye-lashes compliment her. A slight smile is all she can manage.

'Rick's in the kitchen, finishing off the starters and this is Jason; he's a friend of Paul and Mark. We just thought we'd make up the numbers, that's all,' Vicky says.

'That's fine. Hi Jason, nice to meet you,' I say, as I shake his hand.

'Hi Lucy, I've heard a lot about you; it's really nice to meet you,' he says, as he nervously shakes my hand.

'Stop analysing, stop analysing,' I say to myself, as I give him the once-over. Relieved there's no feeling or instant chemistry towards him. Gentle, shy, pale-blue eyes look into mine as his thin lips break out into a welcoming smile, breaking the eye contact as he looks downwards in his shyness. Hands let go as he steps back into his Perspex protective box; a defence mechanism invisible to even his eye.

'Hi Lucy,' Rick says, as he walks into the room and gives me a kiss on the cheek.

'Hi Rick,' I say, feeling comfortable and knowing I'm amongst friends.

'Well, come on, the starters are ready,' Rick says, and leads us into the kitchen-diner room.

'I love this room,' I say, as I look around.

'Thanks Lucy. It was all done before we bought it. A builder bought and really gutted the whole house. It was left to rack and ruin before then and had been empty for about five years.'

It is a lovely room, like a dream kitchen, really bright and airy. The kitchen units are a mix of black gloss and walnut wood with a range in the middle. We are sat at an eight-seat, walnut table with matching chairs that have black leather, padded seats. A brown leather, corner settee dominates the rest of the room and a glossy-black, flat-screen television hangs on the wall. Pure-white, painted walls, fixed spotlights around the whole edge of the floor and ceiling.

'Was this the house you were telling me about, when you were first on about moving from the White House?' I ask Vicky.

'No. I did see one which was a lot cheaper, but by the time we sold the White House as you call it, Rick and I were sure we were going to stay together so we pulled out of buying the other one. This was only thirty grand more expensive and we didn't have to do anything with it; we can concentrate on being a family,' Vicky says.

'It's really lovely,' I say admiringly.

Jason is sat opposite me, Vicky and Rick are sat at either end of the table, Melanie and Susan are sat opposite their husbands.

'Melanie tells me you enjoy writing,' Jason asks, as he smiles warmly at me, though Melanie starts laughing.

'Thanks Melanie. I do enjoy writing; not saying I'm any good at it, but I think it's good to have a hobby,' I say.

'I agree. I used to enjoy writing poetry and I used to do a lot of it when I was at university many years ago. But now I just build and work for Mark,' he says.

I can't help but think that he may be ideal; I mean he must be romantic if he likes poetry, works hard and is good at DIY. Listen to me; I don't even fancy him.

'You should try and pick it up again when you're chilling out,' I say.

'I might do if I find the time,' he smiles.

'You do have the time, now that you're single,' Paul chirps up.

Cheeks warming up with embarrassment as I look across to Jason and see he has gone a little red.

'Okay big mouth, leave it; you're embarrassing both Lucy and I now. Sorry Lucy but now you know why Melanie and Paul make such a lovely couple; they both have big gobs,' Jason squirms.

We laugh as we eat our food. The night is easy; fantastic food, nice wine, great company, and no uneasy, silent moments; no pressure, it is just making up numbers, which I like.

Jason and I find ourselves sat on the corner settee, trying to digest our three-course meal. Jason seems a little awkward and doesn't make me laugh. I like easy-going, fun people; maybe we can be friends. He starts to write drunken poetry on a small notepad and his drunken eyes look into mine as he reads it. He stares a little too much, so I distract him and make my excuses to leave.

'Thanks for a great night,' I say to Rick and Vicky, as I hug them goodbye.

'Open this tomorrow morning,' Rick says, as he passes me a sealed, brown envelope.

'What is it?' I ask, as I take it out of his hand.

'It's a job description for a vacancy at the Liverpool branch. I want you to seriously think about it for a fresh start; you need a change,' Rick says.

'I think you're right. I'll read it tomorrow,' I say, and place it into my bag.

'I didn't really get a chance to tell you, but I've been promoted; splitting my time between Liverpool and Manchester and the branches within that area, so you won't have to put up with me every day. Probably best now that you spend time with me and Vicky outside of work,' Rick says.

'Congratulations. I'm made-up for you. I'll seriously consider it; speak soon,' I say.

'Have you got the poetry I wrote for you,' Jason asks.

'I have; they're here in my bag,' I laugh.

Melanie and Paul walk to the taxi that has pulled up outside the house.

'It was lovely to meet you,' Jason says, as he reaches for a gentle hug and kisses me on the cheek.

I hug him back desperately wanting to feel a shiver down my spine; feel that this is fate and he's the man of my dreams, the love of my life, my soulmate, my all. Oh, pass me the sick bucket.

'It was nice to meet you too, Jason,' I say, as I turn away and walk towards the taxi.

I smile as I get in the taxi; happy there was no magic in the air and knowing it was just really nice to meet someone new.

'Well, he really fancies you,' Melanie squeals, as the taxi pulls away.

'Melanie, that's not true,' I laugh.

'It is. Isn't it Paul?' Melanie nudges him. 'When you went to the toilet before we had dessert, he said that he couldn't believe you were single. He said you were his ideal woman and was going to ask you out again. I told him straight that you want to get to know someone as friends and he was happy with that. He's older than you; made mistakes in the past and like you, he's lived. Can you imagine, we can have dinner parties at each other's houses,' Melanie laughs gleefully.

'Hang on, you've practically married us off already and I don't really know anything about him,' I laugh.

'He is a really decent bloke; he'll treat you really well if you give him a chance,' Paul says.

'Let's just see what happens. I'm happy to be his friend; not sure about anything else,' I say.

Breaking through the bracken and entanglement of the jungle, step out into the wide-open space at the other side of the ninth island, astounded by the tranquillity and feel as I sit down. Look out onto the moonlit waters as the lighted pathway breaks away into darkness. No desire to be forced any further; don't want anything or anyone to control my life or to feel that they know what's best for me. Navy-blue sky has lightened in the early hours of this morning, opening the air and the space around me.

'Right, I'll call you tomorrow,' Melanie says, as the taxi pulls up outside of my house.

'Here's a fiver,' I say, as I hand it over to Melanie.

'Get lost, the taxi will only cost seven quid. We'll get it. You can spend that on a bottle of wine for when I come round and get the gossip about you and Jason,' Melanie laughs.

I smile as I step out of the taxi and close the door. I don't want to read into it too much, as Melanie and Paul are just getting carried away with it; unsure if I even like Jason yet. It's only been seven months since Mike and I split. I just want to take it easy and slowly get to know Jason as a friend, before I even decide whether I really fancy him. Or maybe I should stop thinking altogether and take each day as it comes.

* * *

Cut-glass, grey waters against the early-morning light; spots of sunlight captivated on each wave of rippled water. Gentleness as I reflect and understand where I am; know I have to keep the focus on me and my dreams.

As I post my application for the job at the Liverpool branch, I feel ready to move to the next island I catch sight of. Brighter feel about my future and change in both my personal and work life.

Fragile wings as clear as glass, tipped with redness; gentle, beautiful, the butterfly soulfully lands on my knee. Stillness, calm, elegantly perched with closed wings. Slowly pull my knees towards my chest to take a closer look at the clear wings. Fragile in their exposure, thinly veined and as beautiful as a stained-glass window; delicate body, wings slowly move. Entranced as this fragile creature escapes to freedom, a freedom even I'm not allowing myself to have yet. A freedom I yearn for, freedom from myself. Can't help but look towards the mountain in the distance, just sat behind what will be the tenth island, they seem so near and clear today. It's a magnificent, blue structure, absolute strength and exposure against a backdrop of pale-orange sky. Almost invisible, delicate butterflies with clear-glass wings flutter past, gently floating as they journey forward. Sat in awe as I watch them move with grace and dignity, awash with the wind.

Blossoming trees on the tenth island, flowers as yellow as daffodils. They look so near, as if the journey from this island to the next will be simple. A reminder that my life can still feel like spring, even on the coldest of days during this winter. A red-tipped wing catches my eye as butterflies continue to flutter past. Dare to continue to move as I stand up and look out across the glistening water. Unsure if my boots will protect my feet as I gingerly step forward.

Nerves as immobile as my previous train crash. Sick to my stomach as I contemplate my interview at the Liverpool branch. Nervous, fumbling hands against my lap; fear of failure but also determination, acknowledgement. Racing brain to keep me busy as I mould myself into the seat, thoughts focused on meeting Jason next weekend. Not remembering much about his phone call or even when it was. I used the interview prep as my excuse not to see him sooner. He said he can't wait to see me again, he'd love to get to know me as a friend and see where it goes from there. He's definitely been primed by Melanie; she actually rang me ten minutes after Jason did, but I didn't let on; it makes her happy. But does it make me happy? I definitely don't want to stumble through another relationship for the sake of it, or be with him for everyone else but me.

Stumbling approach to the tenth island, water lapping against my boots as I trudge ahead, slightly burdened. Look back at the cliff's edge, astounded at its disappearance, uncomprehending, sheer disbelief. Collapsed, large pieces of rock heaped at the waters' edge, no longer mountainous in height. Screaming sounds of industrial cranes as the strong arm hoists the rock out of its collapsed state and into large industrial vehicles. Sickness in my thoughts as I watch it all being driven away, removed as if it was all nothing.

Nervous trepidation as I step off the train, relieved to feel the heavy blanket of cold air against my face. Take a deep breath as I catch my reflection against the darkened, glass wall. Fumbling for my ticket, hold it up to the stony-faced man as my eyes meet his emptiness. No expression or emotion or even recognition of life; empty spirit at this early hour. Grasp for breath as I breeze out of the large, clear-glass doors and into the city. Life; feel alive, feel *my* feelings. Grateful I am living in this moment, absorbing the air I breathe. The sky lightens as I wait for guidance from the green man. A safe crossing as the busy traffic comes to a halt to the sound of high-pitched beeping as I cross the road and walk towards the bank.

Look towards the building; it's mountainous in structure. Want to feel my nerves, to deal with them as they come. No longer robotic, I have clarity in my approach as I grip the hard, plastic folder; my safety and preparation for the interview.

Stunned silence as I step onto the tenth island, unable to see it in all its glory; not until I rest my aching body after that exhausting journey. Gratefully sit on the dampened ground, appreciate and know I can only live my life forwards.

Stiff breeze against the nervous heat within my body, relief in my step as I walk out of the bank after that interview; feel shell-shocked and unable to remember how it even progressed. Smile to myself, achievement, confidence, adrenalin running through my body.

Delicate yellow amongst the green; skinny, naked, entwined branches, smooth to the touch. Caress as I admire their beauty, branching off into displays of yellow, blossoming flowers and green leaves. Petals of yellow delicately fall like gentle snowflakes, captured within my grasp as I hold out my hands. Feel as soft and as fragile as pure silk, practically disintegrate when touched; gentle brush as they touch my face. Look up into the sky as streams of yellow fall down, captured within my hair and clothing.

Tread carefully as snow sticks to the ground; slower pace as I walk back towards the train station. Flakes of snow gently falling from the sky, clinging to my clothing.

'Over here, Lucy, in the van,' a familiar voice echoes around me. A sound that is lost within the noise of the city as I near the station.

'Lucy!' Jolted into the pathway as I turn around again and see Jason sat in his works van. I smile as I walk towards him.

'What are you doing here?' he shouts. 'Get in, quick' he urges, as the traffic lights turn to green and he needs to move forward.

I jump into the van and buckle up.

'I've just had my interview and it was bloody awful,' I say.

'I'm sure it wasn't that bad,' he says reassuringly.

'I'll soon find out I suppose,' I sigh.

'You need a coffee, you do,' Jason says, as he looks at me with a concerned look on his face.

'I do need something to get over the shock of it,' I say.

'I know we're not going out till weekend, but let's have a coffee,' Jason suggests.

'Sure, that'll be nice' I say, as I look at him and smile, then lean back into the passenger seat and look out of the window. Struggle to find something to talk about and don't want to stress about that, as I desperately search within my heart and brain; nothing available, no interesting topics of discussion come to mind.

Silence, pure, blank mind as the van suddenly stops in its journey. Jason drives into a parking space. Immediately unbuckle my seatbelt, no desire to look into his eyes. Open the door and step out of the van.

'Come here you,' Jason says, as he pulls me gently towards him and gives me a gentle hug. It's not overpowering which I like, just reassuring. He then ruffles my hair which makes me laugh, but I still don't really *feel* any electricity.

'You get a table and I'll get the coffees,' Jason says, as he holds the door open for me and gently places his hand on my shoulder.

I sit at a table for two with my back towards Jason at the service counter; no idea why I've made the decision to do so but I know it's deliberate.

'There you go,' Jason says, as he places the two coffees on the table and sits down opposite me.

'Thanks,' I say, and immediately pick up the mug of coffee and sip it.

Sat at the table with our coffees, searching for something, but then remember I don't need to search for anything. The most important relationship a person can have is with themselves, so why the hell am I obsessing about Jason and forgetting about me?

Empty chatter and conversation; don't really want to be here but agree to meet at the weekend.

'See you at the weekend,' I say, as Jason walks towards his van and I walk towards home. No desire to be in his company any longer, but not really admitting that to myself. It's as if that information is stuck in the background and not at the forefront of my mind.

Pull on my gloves and button up my coat, relieved the snow hasn't settled on the ground. Slightly downhearted but no idea why. Refocused mind is what I need as I continue to walk home.

Isolation amongst the entanglement of the branches, challenges my desire to be on my own in this place. Turned into a safe haven, surrounded by a beauty that isn't true, soft feeling disappearing within my grasp.

Sharp pain in my right hand, immediately pull away from the branches. Rubbing my hands as I step back in realisation; the branches are no longer elegant in their appearance or touch. Burning embers, white, ashen ground. Emptiness, decay, broken graveyard of foliage. Turn around in every direction; maybe this is it. Am I actually seeing things for what they really are and not what I want them to be?

Feel of warmth and relief as I walk into the house, thankful for central heating. Buzzing mobile phone; rummage in my bag. Four missed calls; buzzing again, Mike's name flashing on the screen, illuminated by a light I don't want to see. A name I don't want to hear or really speak of again. Sit down on the settee, vibrating phone in hand, flashing name in my face. No strength to answer or to protect myself from chaos. Try to remember the strength of detachment as I listen to the voicemails, distraught drunkenness. It's enough to make me realise I want to be on my own for a while longer; don't have enough room for another friend. I won't be meeting Jason at the weekend.

Ash-covered boots, unsupported, uphill climb, clambering using anything I can get hold of. Blackened, fragile branches crumble when touched, suffocating air.

* * *

Fumble with the envelope as I remove the letter; gleeful read as it is an offer for the new job in Liverpool. Definite acceptance, definitive change of direction in my life as I leave the past behind me and look ahead.

Blackened, torched trees; survived the wreckage of a devastating fire, taller than my eyes will allow me to see. Trunks, bleeding black tar, hardening like shattered glass, black ash floating within the air around me. Walk along a clear pathway through the burning timbers, stepping over ground level foliage which has practically disintegrated in the heat. Narrow access opened up, no longer suffocated by the entanglement...

'I still don't know why you'd want to change jobs,' Carol shouts over from the reception desk.

'A change is as good as a rest Carol. I will miss you all but it's just something I have to do,' I shout over, as I try to make myself comfortable, sitting at my workstation.

'Well, better the devil you know, that's what I say, and you're working in the other branches from next week, so won't see you after that,' Carol sighs.

'Had enough of devils to last my lifetime,' I whisper to myself. 'We'll stay in touch Carol; Liverpool isn't that far away.'

Difficult containment of excitement as I serve each customer, knowing new faces will enter my life. Waves of nervousness if I even think about presenting and training personnel on the new document I produced.

Step out of the tall line of tarred trees and into a wide-open space of destruction, blackened soil and fallen trees; dead where they lay. Look beyond the devastation; flourishing trees with leaves of plum-red and golden-brown. Soil as soft as sponge underfoot, sinking feel as I step over the broken, lifeless skeletons of previous jungle foliage. Walking within shadowed darkness, enlightenment ahead as the sun gleams life back into this world.

Look ahead to the upcoming New Year, have faith and hope that my life will get back on track.

Chapter 11

Christmas morning, so peaceful and fun; two words I would never put together, not until I found and understood what peace of mind was. Excitement in each step as I walk downstairs. Wrapped presents in the place the alcoholic used to unconsciously lie. Real smile as I switch on the kettle. Rush of iced air as I open the back door and watch the dog clamber out into the back garden.

Laughter as we open our presents, hugging, loving embrace as six of us come together to celebrate, and for a brief moment I almost forgot their dad passed away five years ago, as if he's here with us; hence six of us and not five. As if this Christmas is one from those yesteryears. Maybe now that Mike has gone, their dad visited for a few brief seconds, as if I almost caught sight of his spirit. I swear he hugged me, reassured all would now be okay and I can't do anything but sit in a daze and watch his outline walk out of the room and out of my view. For a moment the room is empty; smoke-filled haze, blackened tar, smoke-damaged, until the Christmas music playing in the background brings me back to my senses. Judder as I try to bring myself back into today. Distorted view; my vision battling between the smoke-filled haze and the bright, shiny Christmas morning. Yearning for my earlier vision, the six of us, as we used to be. Knowing I have to move forward and snap myself out of my heartbreak. Confused and placing myself on standby, yearn to get this year over with so that I can bounce back into life in the New Year. I really don't know what I think will magically happen once the New Year arrives, yet I daydream the time away … counting the days.

* * *

Restlessly wait in the coffee shop for Vicky, relieved New Year's Eve has finally arrived. Unguarded, wide open body and a mind like a sponge, desperately want to soak up new and exciting experiences. Smiling about nothing in particular as I look out onto the High Street, winter sunshine melting the snow. Bleakness captivated by the rays and the brightly coloured wellingtons, umbrellas, layers of winter clothing as bodies busily huddle past. Laugh out loud as I recognise Andy's clothed body breeze past, pushing a trolley towards his sandwich shop. He must be staying here after all and looks like he's celebrating the New Year right on the High Street. Can't tell you how happy I feel; free spirited glow, amused by everything and nothing.

Sudden captivation by an unknown force; heat, pulling sensation, drawn towards his eyes, magnetic attraction from my soul to his. Racing heart as I feel him penetrate; those eyes are looking right into me, examining my every move.

'Is it me or is it hot in here?' I think to myself; a definitive change in the atmosphere as I fumble, unsure what to do.

He forcefully moves his chair; dramatic declaration, he wants me to know he's there and that I've seen. My god, I can't speak; he seems to be walking over in slow motion. Watch every inch of his body as he moves, a structure of strength, passion and hope. Confidence in his stature, arrogance in his approach, determination in those amazing, green eyes as his mouth breaks out into the most amazing smile. Eyes set ablaze. My heart is beating deeply and my breathing has slowed down so that my breasts practically heave out of my bra.

Completely stuck solid, held down, chained onto my chair, just staring at him, completely speechless; his movements are slow and breathless. My mind is blank, I feel as if I should be wearing a virginal, white nightgown, which is see-through and cut too low at the cleavage and clings to them like the breasts were sewn into the gown. He'll stand before me, take me into his arms and carry me out of this coffee shop, carry me out of this world I'm in, carry me out of this jungle, lay me down amongst the sheltering foliage. Kneel beside my surrendering, helpless body. Trembling as I lie there in complete awe of him, slow movements as he pulls down my gown to reveal the paleness of my naked skin. Flesh that wants to be taken. Forbidden embrace, pure nakedness as he looks into my eyes, searching for lips that want to be found, no longer able to hold back from this feeling.

'Hi Lucy, sorry I'm a bit late,' Vicky says, as she breathlessly comes bounding into the coffee shop, frozen to the core. Red-nosed coldness, warmed with maroon, knitted hat and scarf. Shell-shocked, unable to answer, I glance over towards the energy that's verging into unbearable.

'Sorry Vicky, I've got to go. I'll ring you later,' I say, as I stand up from my chair in a bit of a daze. Confused.

'But you've not finished your coffee; can't you stay for a bit, I've only just arrived?'

Look over and watch as he stands up to put on his black, winter coat. Smouldering, hypnotic glare, captivating desire as he brazenly stares over at me.

'Really sorry Vicky, just going for some fresh air. Get a coffee and I'll be back in a bit,' I say, as I put on my coat and place my handbag strap on my shoulder. As I turn around, he opens the door for me.

'Thanks,' I say, as I walk out of the door and smile at him. I can feel him behind me, a towering strength.

'Excuse me,' he shouts.

I turn around, confronted by his force and he gently touches my face, takes me into his strong hold and gazes into my eyes. Melt into him as if I've been waiting for this moment all of my life. I turn around and he's stood there smiling at me.

'Your belt is hanging on the floor,' he says.

I look down and see that I hadn't tied the belt around my waist; I was in too much of a hurry to get out of the coffee shop.

'Thanks,' I say, as I tie the belt.

'Can I give you my mobile number,' he asks.

'Sure.'

'I take it you're single then?' he asks.

'Yes I am.' I get my phone out of my bag. 'What's your name?'

'Cain,' he answers.

'Cain,' I smile to myself, as I put his name and number into my phone.

'What's your number?' he asks.

Jolt through my heart as he stands over me, protective feel, un-suffocating. Places his hands on each of my shoulders, stops me from plummeting to the ground.

'I feel as if I know you from somewhere, but I can't think where. Text or ring me later and I'll take you out,' he says, as he gently squeezes my shoulders.

Feeling dazed as I hypnotically gaze at his hands, 'Okay,' I say, as he releases me and walks away.

Vicky watches from inside the coffee shop. I wave at her and point over towards the bank to let her know I'll only be a minute. Beaming, electrifying smile as I think about Cain and the way he makes me feel. Thoughts on how he knows me, acknowledgement I already know him but not sure how or if we've ever actually physically met before.

Try to keep my enormous grin under control as I walk towards the coffee shop. Vicky looks bemused, sipping coffee, examining me with her eyes.

'Do you want another coffee Vicky?' I ask, as I walk into the coffee shop.

'And a cake; surprise me,' she says, with a smile.

Uncontrollable beam as I stand at the service counter. Have my back to Vicky as I struggle to contain this joy.

'You can't contain yourself can you,' Vicky laughs, as I place the tray of cake and coffees on the table.

'I feel like an idiot; don't know what the hell he's done to me,' I laugh.

'You do know he went to school with us don't you?'

'I don't remember him, but my memory isn't as good these days.'

'Well I remember. Cute, dark-skinned, always hanging around and I know he always admired you. We were too busy laughing to notice. It's good that friendship and laughter were the most important thing to us in those days.'

'It still is to some degree Vicky, we've just got to work a bit harder to make sure it doesn't get lost. I think I vaguely remember him, but I was sure he had died in an accident a few years back; it must have been someone else.'

Sip coffee and eat cake on New Year's Eve with a great, non-judgmental friend who's experienced real life, knows and understands herself, and me for that matter. What more can I ask for?

'Don't you be worrying about Melanie trying to pair you up with Jason; you do what you want to do. May not be a bad thing moving to Liverpool to work; live your life for yourself,' Vicky assures.

'I intend to Vicky, thanks for reminding me,' I say, with a smile.

Live life for myself … do I even know what that means? Do I really even understand that concept? To live life is an achievement in itself. To wake up every day and to live in that moment knowing what *I* want to do. Imagine trying to live each day for myself; well, not trying yet imagine doing just that. To wake up knowing who I am and what I like to do, want to do, without pressure; without having to please somebody else. Without having to put *me* to one side because a certain person does not want me to do what *I* want. They want me to live my life for them; to please them and no one else.

I am actually praying that the New Year will bring me everything I dream of, everything I want, but I've got to step out of my comfort zone; a magnificent leap into the unknown. I can't sit and wait daydreaming the good times; I have to get up and get hold of life; shake it, wake it up. Wake myself up; promise myself I will, and not an empty type of promise like a failed diet. The last chocolate bar that's never the last. This is it, it has to be, there's no other way.

Chapter 12

The present moment is the only moment available to us, and it is the door to all moments.
Thich Nhat Hanh

Each strike is like a new awakening; twelve strikes of time as the New Year beckons me to move forward with my life. Look out towards the mainland; no dramatic entrance onto it, no applauding crowd or fat lady singing. Just a simple realisation that I completely neglected and mistreated the one person I should take care of the most ... *me*. A life without unacceptable behaviour from other people, filled with sensible boundaries that offer me the freedom I've been yearning for.

Fireworks enlighten the sky; a blinding light catapulted into the whole atmosphere. Electrifying noise and drama magnifying the night, it's then I see the old, wooden rowing-boat tied to a tree that stands alone at the edge of this island. Knocking wood as the boat beats against the trunk. Look back but don't stare at where I've journeyed from. Disappearing jungle foliage; flattened ground as the tidal sea gushes towards me. Recaptured islands now settled under water, no longer in existence within this atmosphere. Blue moon fixed like a torched light in the midnight sky, fireworks ablaze, a backdrop for the realisation the cliff's edge has finally disintegrated along with the *Field of Ignorance*. No longer haunting me from afar; the whole sky has opened up into a blaze of glory. Hold on to the trunk of the tree, protected by huge formations of rock that jut out from the seabed with their razor-sharp edges. The sea is the colour of black ink, reflecting against the moonlight. I watch as it crashes into the rocks and then sucks itself back out; right out as far as the eye can see. A daunting, thunderous sound as it storms towards the rocks and crashes up against them. Intense sea breeze, vigorously knocking into the rowing-boat. If I don't move now, I might not make it back to shore. Step into the boat and immediately sit down on the little wooden seat. Loosen the knot in the rope, keep it wrapped around the trunk. I can feel the force of the water, trying to push the boat to the shore. I take one more look around before I let go. Smile as I appreciate where I've been, thankful that I'm awake and alive, not just breathing or existing. Sigh of relief as I let go of the rope and feel the immediate force of the boat being pushed to the shore and use the oars to keep me in a straight line. As I near the shore, daylight starts to show itself from behind the jungle trees.

Swept away by tidal current towards the mainland, feels like an eternity as I watch the sunrise set the whole sky on fire, blazon in deep red as the pure glow stretches out across the atmosphere. Water sleeps within the shadows of the darkened redness, ripples exaggerate within the strokes of my rowing, then lose themselves against the dark-red, shadowed water. Black outline of the mainland overshadows as I near; look back towards the deep, hazy glow of the sun. Magnificent power as it magically magnifies colour into the air I breathe. Amazing as it filters through the trees and across the mainland. Low-flying birds silent in their approach as they sweep across the water; sit in awe as I watch their wings move in slow motion. Beautiful embrace of flight as they empower the atmosphere with the strength of each movement. Breathless motion of freedom as they glide out towards another land.

Step out of the rowing-boat, take hold of the old piece of rope that's tangled up at the bottom and tie it to a wooden post that is sticking out of the soiled mainland.

There's no sign of Mike, but he's cleared the way for me and I walk through the clearance within the jungle branches. The ground is bone-dry. Struggle to walk up a steep pathway, hold onto the large leaves that feel like hardened leather.

Uneasy feel as I hear distant cries, squealing and chanting. Off the beaten track I slow my pace; silent approach as I struggle to move through the foliage. The twisted, jungle roughage comes to an abrupt end and opens up into a large area of clearance. A humungous tree grows out from the middle of the clearance. Definitely the tree of all trees; never seen anything like it before, not whilst being here. Bulking roots curve outwards and upwards before growing back underground, creating a half circle like an opening into the tree. I daren't step out from where I am hiding; sit down amongst the foliage, partially hidden behind large, twisted branches.

Squealing troop of baboons come bounding out from nowhere, congregated within the half-circled trunk of the tree. Aggressive assertion, close-set eyes, long muzzles, powerful jaws threaten each other. Thick fur protects their thick skin as they fight, determined to be the first to climb that tree. One large baboon is thundering around, pacing back and forth, and preventing the others from getting near. The pacing baboon seems to be ringleader, the most determined of them all. Clearly snarling and showing its canine teeth. I watch as it takes a run up and pulls itself up the tree branches. Completely shows its pure-red backside, ferociously pacing along the thick, tangled branches. I watch as excrement falls out of the redness and into its hand, heave as it starts to eat it as the others look on.

I watch as four baboons try to prance up the tree, sticking their red backsides up in the air, but the fierce baboon prevents them from getting near the top, throwing excrement, snarling and thumping against the branches. It doesn't make sense to me at all, so I sit and continue to watch from the sidelines. Shocked to witness such aggression, venomous, bitter taunts, bullying. It's then I notice the long, blonde hair on the pacing baboon and I realise it's Jenny. Out of control, unable to contain or understand her own emotions, or look within herself, all she can do is punish others to falsely increase her self-esteem, to feel powerful. I then recognise the other baboons as they retreat to the half-circle, no longer showing their redness and it makes me realise I've been spending too much time worrying about nonsense going on in work, spending too much of my precious time worrying about people who don't really belong in my life. People who have nothing better to do but fight to get to the top of that tree, no matter what it takes and they don't care what they have to do to get there, and don't care who they hurt or humiliate.

It's at that point I stand up and step back into the jungle; I decide to keep my distance; keep away from the jungle tree and the baboons. But also not let it spoil the great times I have with the great people I have met through work, still meet, to know as usual it is only a very small percentage that spoil it for the majority. And appreciate the lesson I have been given, to understand life and to not feel any bitterness towards people who hurt as they are hurting themselves, no one else. Smile to myself, as I take it all in, see it for what it is. Walk back towards the track where things are straight-forward, just a simple path to follow. I know where I am when I stick to a simple path. The warmth of the sun and enchanting light saturates the ground and the air that surrounds me as it rises in the light-blue sky. The path opens and I see a clearance in the distance which will lead me out of the jungle and into my new life.

Sit down at the side of the path and take a deep breath as I walk into the Liverpool branch on my first day in my new job. Beaming heart as I learn new elements of work, feel challenged and proud, seriousness diminished as personalities shine through, though I don't seem to have time to even think about my family, never mind see them, feel so confused. Also know that work is not my top priority. I am. I will cope, work hard. I even like the people I work with and I want to have fun, want to have real, gut-wrenching laughter in my life, every day. As I step out of the branch after my first day, I am greeted by Melanie and Vicky. I have gut-wrenching laughter in my life and in my heart when I'm with them, though I really wish John was here, laughing, joking, happy to be back together and I feel guilty that I'm not with John, as if he needs my support and I'm not here for him, and as I unlock the front door to *my* home, it feels safe, calm and happy; everything is at ease.

Stand up and walk towards the opening that will take me away from this place, this burden. Enraptured by the beautiful song as birds joyfully chirp, surrounded by butterflies, delicately flickering within dance, showing their burnt-orange, red and black coloured wings. Relieved, deep breaths, slight nervousness as I step into the small clearance.

Brought to a complete stop, I'm prevented from stepping out from the opening in the jungle. Hands touch and feel an invisible, hardened encasement. Frantically feel upwards as the sun gleams from outside this barrier. Rays from the sun embrace the outline of the Perspex, a familiar and recognisable structure. Step back in amazement as I digest the realisation I'm trapped inside this huge Perspex bubble that's encasing the whole atmosphere. Perspex reaches up higher than the jungle trees and encases everything within it. Look beyond the bubble and I see familiar faces; distraught, comforting embrace, huddled together, brought together in mourning. Look down underfoot, decayed, rotting foliage.

Slimy, dying, stench filled air, bleeding guts from rotten, unidentifiable corpses, unable to escape from this place. Nowhere to go but backwards as I try to push against the barrier, knowing I'll only exhaust myself if I try any longer. Acceptance and logical thinking as I run back towards the place I'm trying to break away from. Splattered rot underfoot, encasing my whole body with stench and filth as I run as fast as I can back into the depths of understanding.

Frantic, haunting memories of running into my *Field of Ignorance*; the only noise is from the splattering sounds as each step touches the rotting ground. Pounding steps that are slowing; exhaustion within my breathing as I come to a halt at the edge of a sunken pit, huge in size. Depths of despair as a single island sits in the centre of it all. Look out at a hunched figure, sat there, with head in hands. Can't see clearly from here, so I walk out amongst the deep-seated, pit-filled rot. A heavy heartbeat, beating against the back of my throat, as the filth soaks around my legs. An energised, squelching sensation; frightened as I approach the figure. Dressed in the same clothing; jump out of my skin as the figure turns to look up at me. It is me, looking up at *me*. A fragile handheld out. I touch and hold it as the figure stands up and we face each other for the first time, in this place. Real recognition as we walk hand in hand. Confused and unsure, all I can do is allow myself to follow this other being.

I hear the familiar sound of knocking. Rowing-boat tied to a post, oars resting inside, rocking in the clear, restful waters. Gently step inside the boat.

Gliding, pure reflections of enraptured trees within the waters; gentleness, and slow movement as the oars touch and enter the water. Eyes catch sight of strong hands gripped to each oar. A picture-perfect world. Stillness. Look in awe as Cain smiles; sheer strength throughout his whole body as the rowing-boat journeys within the trees. Smile as I look back towards the encasement of the jungle. Tall trees that act as a screen, hidden world. Acknowledge freedom as warmth of the sun enlightens our faces. The boat effortlessly moves as Cain rows with magnificence; strong arms pushed and then pulled towards his strength and structure.

Cain urges me to look within the reflected waters as he rows me to another land. Reflections and realisation that send a shudder through my entire being. Absolute horror as I instantly rewind back to when I was on the stage to collect my award for being the new writer of the year. My dream, my desire, a life goal I could focus on just for me, rather than my life being centred on unhealthy aspects of everybody else. The tightness, a grip around my neck … the life was being strangled out of my body ... my life. I fought against it, writhing around on my bed, holding onto the strong grip that was taking my final breath. I can feel the energy now, I can still hold onto that emotion as it spiralled out, leaving only pitiful sparks and flakes of final thoughts; thoughts that were focused on everybody else's lives, meaningless conversations, work- related nonsense. Left alone to realise I hadn't been living my life, merely existing for everyone else. I am, or I was, a mother of four beautiful children, yet none have been in my thoughts, only John, very briefly. As if he was caught up in my bitter end somehow and the fragments of energy left within were fizzing. As if my children had been erased from my life, as I tried to make sense of what was going on, too wrapped up in everything else, not realising I had died, passed over, but not completely. Not until I realised where I truly am and that moment has only arrived now, here. My body lay in bed, as if it took a while for my spirit to leave my side. Mike sat on the floor, sat staring in disbelief, moving ever so close to my empty decaying embodiment, inching himself forward; harsh reality of what he had done but desperate to wake me up.

Cain points towards the nearing land, I can sense the energy from my spirit, the spirit that left me behind so it could comfort loved ones; left me to make sense of the unknown as

I desperately tried to make my way back to a world that no longer existed to me. A golden glow, an outline of recognition returned to finally merge with me again. Reflected waters take me back to the time of my death and a fire that was started some time later, as if the killer desperately tried to hide what they had done. An empty body dragged from room to room, uncertain how to dispose.

Golden light, warm energy as the boat finally halts; a hazy, welcoming spirit beckons me to finally accept and emerge. Assurance that my loved ones have been taken care of, that responsibility was taken away from my vision and emotion. I had my own journey; a journey of realisation that I was no longer alive, am no longer alive. Strong hold of Cain as he comforts the realisation from within. Sent to me, to help ease me out of my spiralling desperation and confusion; finally leaving the jungle and settling into my resting place as my body is taken and mourned. Cries, recognised sorrow as loved ones say their goodbyes. My energy lives on, lives beyond my life with them, urging me to learn from my previous life somehow. To live life for *me*. To not allow anyone to interfere or control my journey. As if there will be a next time. Leave behind the meaningless taunts, only the warmth of love exists now. Happiness in my heart, learnings for a new beginning ...

A soothing, enchanting light … a warm embrace enveloped in love and kindness. Love is all that exists now, in this place. Taken back to visualise the love and laughter I shared with my ex-husband John, the father of my four beloved children. The husband I would have spent my lifetime with if the cruelty of illness had not taken him away from us all. Senses filled with a powerful, deep emotion. As warm as a new Spring, John and I would lie on our picnic blanket and build daisy chains; lie in each other's arms and smile deeply as the warmth of the sun melted into our skin. Smile, as I remember walking along the beach with John, holding hands; and if I close my eyes I can still hear the roar of the sea, still feel the softness of the pure, white sand and hear the sound of laughter. During glorious, spring evenings, John and I would stay to capture the redness of the sun as it set in the early evening sky; wrap ourselves up and protect ourselves against the enchanting sea breeze. I can't help but appreciate how John and I brought up our four beautiful children, remember their first smile, first word, first walk, as if it were yesterday. Appreciate what it feels to love and be loved. The precious moments we shared as a family, the simple things like colouring books, painting, singing nursery rhymes. And I can't help but cry when I think about the school run, excited, welcoming smile, when John or I picked them up from school; then we would go for a walk in the park, play on the swings and slides. I loved our family holidays; a visit to the zoo; the fair. Birthday parties were more than perfect days, blowing out the candles, excitedly open presents, hugs and kisses. Christmas. What can I say about Christmas? The build-up was so exciting; uncontrollable enthusiasm, hyperactivity from September onwards; letters to Santa, excited laughter; playing in the snow and building a snowman; we were a perfect family. Comforting embrace, aching for the feel of John's strong hold; he was a fantastic father, so attentive and had no fear of tears and tantrums. He embraced their individuality, yearned for them to have and to feel freedom. We all loved walking the dog; the only time I witnessed John losing his temper was when the children started tormenting the dog or dressing up the dog in a ridiculous outfit. But you know, John was the biggest child of them all, he'd go out and buy water pistols, water balloons; be the first to play on bouncy castles, trampolines. The only time there was a real clash of personalities was during homework, not wanting to do homework; mathematical equations that will never ever be used in the real world. But he always made it up to them when they went out fossil hunting, crabbing, fishing, collecting berries, growing sunflowers; using petals to make perfume.

Me, what about me? Who was I, do I even remember? I do pre-Mike. I loved music, singing to music, that's how I met John, karaoke night in a club. I was born to sing more than I was to write. Freedom, I loved freedom, driving my car. I was obsessed with the sunset, sunrises, the moon, stars, butterflies, birds.

And as I lie in the comfort of John's spirit, my beloved soulmate, I sense he will not remain with me. He has already set himself free from this place; I need to remain for a while longer to evaluate and accept so I can learn and move forward. And what about my son John, is he here or still with his brother and sisters. That is what I need to know before I leave here. I can't see or feel him, he feels as disconnected from me as my other children. I want to see them, feel them one last time, hug them; tell them I am okay; they will be okay. I can hear familiar laughter, playful banter … I can see, I have to see. On the beach, they're all there but I can't quite make out if all four are there; reminiscing, taking themselves back to their younger years when all six of us were together. We loved the beach, they loved kite flying, playing a game of cricket, and paddling in shallow water. Frisbees, they're playing with the old, red Frisbee now, launching it and the dog is there, going wild, crazy. Stan. Don't ask why he is called Stan, but I was so sure Stan was no longer with them, as I'd seen Mike strangling the life out of some type of animal and I presumed it was Stan. Mike is definitely not here, nowhere near me, I know that for sure; he's gone….

Tears of joy, I feel contentment, so happy to see my children; to know they are happy, free. I would give anything to hold them, hold their hands. Laugh, talk and ask how their day has been; console any worries, be silly, giddy; blow bubbles and watch as the bubbles float and carry themselves effortlessly until they disintegrate before your very eyes. Enchanted by their silhouettes, dancing wistfully as the sea breeze enraptures their spirits. They're waving, suddenly waving and shouting across to where I'm standing. A sickness overwhelms the pit of my stomach; a heartbeat, brought back to life. I feel as if I've fallen from a great height and the landing has suddenly cut me open, restarted my inner being. They've seen me, I can't believe they see me, they know I'm here. Running, screaming with such intent, they're coming, running with all they've got to reach me. They've missed me, they want me; feeling overwhelmed, felt as if I'd never see them again … ever; and as their panic-stricken shadows close in on where I lay, I know they're here….

Here, where is here? Distorted view, distorted memories, sudden confusion … burning fire, burning house. Mike, he's sat in the middle of the fire, on *his* chair, the one where he loses himself. Saturated in alcohol, swigging it down, allowing it to flow into his gut with no care for himself or anyone for that matter. Absolute arrogance as burning embers, roaring flames engulf the room. No emotion, nothing; he's ready to die. Flickering eyes, confusion as I awake from unconsciousness. Pain, I feel pain, tightness around my neck, my head, pain in my head; blood, blood is everywhere, a wound on my head, the back of my head. Smoke, I smell smoke, scared to cough in case Mike realises I'm not dead. My spirit has seeped back into my body, allowing me to see, to know for sure. John, John's lying near to where I am, no … please, not John. Stretch my arm out, feel him, feel for life. A groan, very faint groan; he is alive, he's here with me, fighting for his life as I am. Urgency, real sense of urgency, time is fading, strength diminishing. But we're alive, we will make it out of here alive. My spirit left my body, I definitely felt it spiral out, left alone … but I made it back, I fought my way back. Even when the clearance to escape was taken away from me I never gave up. My love for my children saved me, kept me strong, kept me alive to return, to here, now. Stan, I can hear Stan barking, left out as usual; Mike had no care for Stan … Stan is alive. We are alive, help has arrived, I can hear the sirens, I can hear the sound of rescuers entering the house, they are here for John and I ... Mike has gone, he definitely has, I know he has, I sense it. But we are alive....

Notes and acknowledgement

This book was published electronically on KDP in February 2015. I decided to make it available as a paperback in 2024 as I was getting ready to publish another 2 books.

I have moved on from this style of writing and learnt a lot, but I didn't want to rewrite this, I wanted to honour it as my debut.

I first had the idea of writing this as a TV script. I could visualise a woman standing on a stage, accepting an award and as she stood there gasping and cooing, the titles for the gritty drama were rolling across the TV screen.

The woman then found herself lying in bed in the grottiest bedroom, inside a dingy flat and was devastated when she realised her time on that stage was just a silly dream.

This book is dedicated to all those who lost themselves in this world, trying to please others.

Printed in Great Britain
by Amazon